TRUTH OR LYON

The Lyon's Den Connected World

Katherine Bone

Dragonblade Publishing, Inc. is an imprint of Kathryn Le Veque Novels, Inc.
P.O. Box 23
Moreno Valley, CA 92556
ceo@dragonbladepublishing.com

Produced in the United States of America

First Edition October 2023
Print Edition

ARE YOU SIGNED UP FOR DRAGONBLADE'S BLOG?

You'll get the latest news and information on exclusive giveaways, exclusive excerpts, coming releases, sales, free books, cover reveals and more.

Check out our complete list of authors, too!

No spam, no junk. That's a promise!

Sign Up Here

www.dragonbladepublishing.com

Dearest Reader;

Thank you for your support of a small press. At Dragonblade Publishing, we strive to bring you the highest quality Historical Romance from some of the best authors in the business. Without your support, there is no 'us', so we sincerely hope you adore these stories and find some new favorite authors along the way.

Happy Reading!

CEO, Dragonblade Publishing

Other Lyon's Den Books

PROLOGUE

A young gentleman of a great estate fell desperately in love with a great beauty of exceedingly high quality, till it was a crime to kiss any woman else. Beauty palls with possession. She disdains him for being tired with that for which all men envied him, and, in a word, this match took the most terrible of appearances, and nothing in nature is so ungrateful as storytelling against the grain.

—The Morning Post

Mayfair, April 1815

"WHAT SHOULD I do? What ought I to say?" Miss Parthenia Steere paced the distance between the bookcase and a reading chair situated near the bow window of Mr. Beaumont's library. What should have been a joyous occasion, a ball boasting frippery and flattery, felt heavy and cumbersome, making her desire to be elsewhere. It wasn't easy being the eldest daughter of a viscount, with two younger sisters dependent on her marital status. The part she played had advantages and disadvantages, some easier to decode than others. *'Duty is all,'*—the mantra of the *ton*—was hard to digest when the moniker *'spinster'* would soon be attached to your name.

And yet—

She had never been kissed.

Whatever my faults, I am not a deceiver. Why, I have never had motive to lie or fabricate my affections before. But this . . . the fact that I do not love the man my parents desire me to marry calls for resourcefulness. It is an urgent matter, a matter of the heart, a mission to secure my freedom. And the very reason I am hiding.

She was not a quitter.

Handel's score Water Music broke through her woolgathering, the lyrical notes drifting softly through the closed door. The set, played with peak talent, afforded her an occasional breath taken by the flutist.

Oh, to be talented and led to follow that occupation.

Mrs. Beaumont's Rout had attracted a company of personages: The Duke and Duchess of Roxburgh; Earl of Westmorland, Lord and Lady Amhurst; the Austrian Ambassador; Lord and Lady Ennismore; the Marquiss and Marchioness of Winchester; the Earl and Countess of Harrington; the Earl and Countess of Manners; Lord and Lady Borringdon; and Count Beroldingen, Chamberlain to the King of Wirtemberg. A fine assembly. The expected crush coincided with another ball at Hertford House to her dismay, however, delaying the arrival of her guests, which was not so unusual a circumstance, given the size of Town.

Awkwardness of the moment, however, offered Thenie a moment to slip away from the luster of ormolu lights into Mr. Beaumont's private library, the incapsulated room with endless books and overstuffed chairs and reading nooks offered longed for respite from the expectations of family and friends.

There, away from those she loathed to disappoint—Mama, Papa, and her twin sisters Augusta and Delphi—she scrutinized the room, then approached an enclosed bookcase to pluck a volume of Shakespeare from the beveled glass. The crisp binding of the old tome grounded her, while turning the pages was an indulgence that eased her spinning mind.

Act One, Scene Two of Hamlet. *"Frailty, thy name is woman.'"* She lowered the tome. "Isn't that the truth." Though she was determined not to fall into that category, tears filled her eyes as she continued to read on. "'She married. O most wicked speed!'" A good woman did not to read this section out loud. *'To post with such dexterity to incestuous sheets, it is not nor it cannot come to good; but break, my heart. For.'* "'I. Must. Hold. My. Tongue.'"

Was that not what the *ton* expected?

But how can I remain silent when my heart cries out for an intangible thing I don't even recognize? What is love? How does one go about finding it?

Papa was in the process of making arrangements for her to marry Lord Reginald Boothe, and time was running out. He was a good man, of course, a rising intellect in political circles. Destined for Parliament. She paused, her finger drumming on the page while she ruminated over the contrast between herself and Hamlet's Gertrude. Her situation was turbulent, to be sure. Nevertheless, she felt no guilt. Experienced no jealousy. She'd done nothing to warrant Boothe's animosity. But would she end up like Gertrude, electing betrayal—defying Papa's generosity, and rejecting Boothe's compassion for the sake of her own selfishness?

"Oof!" She stamped her foot. "What am I to do?"

Frustrated, she slapped the book closed and restored it to the shelf. Time had run out and her situation must be remedied some way or the other. Preferably seeing her unattached to Boothe by night's end.

But how could such a miracle be achieved?

"A kiss." *I have never been kissed before. Does one need to feel an attachment first? Is there a particular method?* She tapped her nose, deep in thought. "Is there a way to practice kissing a man without causing a scandal?"

No. No. An upright woman would not dare think of it, let alone commit such a thing.

"Kissing a man risks the hue and cry before all and sundry. Scandalous!" Few things escaped the *ton.* And worse . . . The dismantling of reputations destroyed young women's prospects. She sagged into an overstuffed chair. "I *am* doomed."

Another set commenced, the harmony penetrating the room, the immediacy heightening her resolve. "I have but one choice left."

I must tell the truth. Admit my foolhardiness. Stand my ground. I am not destined to marry. Not yet, anyway. I desire love, not convenience and courtesy. "If I am to retain any dignity at all—" She raised her fist. A line had to be drawn in the sand. She must fight for survival, even if it meant ambling aimlessly toward ruin.

What would her cousin do?

Lady Charlotta "Lottie" Grey had found every happiness in reuniting with her childhood sweetheart, Lord Septimus Grey. The romantic inside of Thenie envied their romance. They had married and taken the Tour, gone these many months. *How adventurous!* No. Settling for a marriage of convenience was no longer possible. It did not appeal. She had seen how love transformed two people. How they became one and the same. But what was she to do? Unlike Lottie, she had no long-lost love to reclaim, no deep affections at the ready.

She was ill-prepared for what lay ahead.

Gow's band embroidered the cords of Handel's melodic strains with the talent they were known far and wide for, a stark reminder that this night was far from over.

A plank in the floor creaked.

She whipped around, fretful she'd been observed, cautiously seeking to ensure that she was, indeed, alone. *Fool hardy, girl. What if someone had overheard the private discussion, she had had with herself? Talk of kissing would surely wag a few tongues.*

Drat! She had a habit of getting herself into a fix. Had she erred again? She should not have sequestered herself in the library among the Beaumont's forest of books. She'd been drawn to the familiarity, remnants of tobacco and lemon and leather, hypnotized like a frightened doe eager to escape its oncoming slaughter.

Mrs. Beaumont's balls were grand diversions, amusements Thenie looked forward to with ambitious fervor. With one exception. Being sold on the meat market was not among them, the uncertainty, fear, and callous disregard for her wants and desires mounting. Boothe deserved the truth. He deserved love, an eager partner—as did she and everyone else tied by marital bonds.

Thenie wanted what her cousins, Lottie and Grey had, what Mama and Papa had.

"I am determined, come what may, that my life will not be ruined by a kiss."

The floor creaked behind her. She turned, coming face-to-face with Boothe, his brows furrowing. "Who have you kissed, Miss Steere?"

CHAPTER ONE

If a man of any delicacy were to attend the discourses of the young fellows of this age, they would believe there were none but prostitutes to make the objects of passion. So true it is of the modern pretenders to gallantry. They set up wits in this age, by saying when they are sober, what they spoke only when they were drunk. But Cupid is not only blind, but dead-drunk. He has lost all his faculties: else how should Celia be so long a maid with that agreeable behavior? Corinna, with that uprightly wit? Cassia, with that heavenly voice? Such is the fallen state of love, that few hardly have little encouragement to persevere.

—The Morning Post

Athens, February 1815

"HUNT IS NOT here, *Afenticó.*"

Spencer Wright-Smythe, Baron of Kilverstone, shot an irritated look at his assistant. "How many times have I told you, Baros, I am not your boss?"

The stocky man snorted, his mischievous expression filled with mirth. "Ample times, *Afenticó.*"

His frustration mounted, even though he knew this was one of Baros's daily games. "Spencer, blast you. At the very least, Smythe."

"Yes, *Patron*."

"Alternating tongues changes nothing. We are comrades, you and I. I am not, nor have I ever been or ever will be your boss."

"My wages say otherwise."

The man had a point, though he hated to admit it. Yet, Baros was more than an associate. *Devil take the man!* He was the only person in Athens that Spencer *could* trust, and he desired to reward that connection, nurturing a bond that spanned centuries of antiquated artefacts. Few shared his passion for the past—most Athenians preferring to make ends meet without the interference of foreigners. And the women . . . while alluring, come-hither and habit-forming, their interests in the here and now, lacked the intellect and sense of adventure he yearned to share with a wife.

He shook off his instinctive desires and centered his attention on the Parthenon, putting this moment to memory. The sun beat down on Athena's temple, the glinting light obscuring Spencer's view of the Marbles, priceless ancient renderings attached to the crown which had fascinated him since his days at Cambridge under Professor Bertrand Walcot's instruction. Not surprisingly, the fanciful ideas of his youth to sail to the Ottoman Empire and trek across ancient Greece fueled his soul, stoking a rare fire deep in his belly. By rights, he should be ambling throughout Kilverstone, executing his duties, and paying far more attention to his tenants than marble hewn by long-dead expert craftsman.

Nevertheless, here he was scrutinizing the vandalized perfection he'd only imagined in his uneducated stupor at Cambridge. Here, feasting on priceless wonders, his miseries and desires fading into oblivion, time melded into one firmament, ceasing to exist. The meticulous precision of a sculptor's chisel releasing images from stone quite easily forgotten.

And yet they live on. They continue to fascinate, to lure people from afar, to be the stuff that dreams are made of.

Where was the proof of *his* existence, like the temple that over-looked Athens before him, crying out that legendary Greeks once walked the Earth?

Curse this blasted yearning to leave something of myself behind, something lasting and pure like the colossal construction before me. That would entail marriage, putting aside his rakish ways, and loving a real human being rather than one emerging from stone.

But how did a man perform such a miracle so far away from civilized society?

Only one of several devoted scholars, he felt a kinship to the Greeks, and even more so now, given the years of war plaguing the United Kingdom. Though Napoleon had never reach England's shores—in good part to Lord Nelson's navy—the Greeks had not been as fortunate. The Ottoman had decimated Athens. And to break the Greek spirit, they had destroyed the center of Athena's temple.

Nonetheless, Athens had persevered, refusing to lose its heart and soul to war and diplomacy.

And neither would he.

Standing before the colossal remnants of Athena's shrine and the entrance that once led to her forty-two-foot statue, long-since destroyed, he knew what he truly searched for would continue to elude him. His exertions detailing each piece Reverend Philip Hunt and Thomas Bruce, 7th Earl of Elgin, had taken from the Ottomans, authenticating and sketching the exquisite sculptures adorning the temple's facade, and his habit of taking on dangerous assignments no longer seemed to excite him.

Instead, everything was a bore.

Nor would he find Hunt—as he'd been tasked to do—who had enthused ambitious Scotsman Elgin—ambassador to Constantinople—to seek profits from the ancient world, its literature and arts.

"Keep watch," he said, realizing how long it had been since he'd responded to Baros. Detailing his own miseries and the reverend's greedy vandalization of the temple served no purpose whatsoever. But one thing was certain. "Hunt's attempts to elude me beggar belief. I will die an old man before he is found."

"Hunt's men are loyal. They alert him whenever we seek permission to ascend the acropolis."

A cost of at least five guineas a day to scale the massive mount.

Aggravated by the situation, Spencer grumbled, cursing the futility of their endeavors. His attempts to verify the firman Elgin insisted he'd obtained from the Ottomans to study and export broken pieces of the Athenian temple were intercepted at every turn.

"Stop worrying, boss." Baros offered a broad smile. "You have me."

"Brilliant." A lot had happened in the three years they'd worked together, much of which he couldn't confess to genteel company. Baros knew everyone and if there was a way to get to Hunt, his companion would find it. None of that changed the truth, however. Greece had fallen to the Ottomans. Control motivated bias. "I have orders to interview Hunt, but he will not appear as long as he knows that we are here."

"Then we must find another way to obtain an interview."

"He has avoided every tactic."

Men like Elgin and Hunt came to conquer and to strip history for selfish gain, though their finances for such endeavors were nearing an end. For this reason, he'd been sent by the British government to appease the Ottomans' concerns and discover whether legal means had been exhausted before Elgin and Hunt began dismantling Athena's temple.

Athens had once been a thriving community, its history and people chronicled in myth and legend. Ottoman invasion, however, enslaved and gutted the heart of Athenian pride. And now, Elgin and Hunt deepened the wound, robbing Greece's soul.

"Boss."

Gazing at the metopes, he pondered anew the talent and time it had taken Greek sculptors to capture motion and sound and life from the depths of the marbles. The stones beautifully chronicled festivities celebrated in daily life. "What is it?" he asked.

"*Koita ekei.*"

He ignored Baros's lapse, allowing the man his fun. There was only so much daylight left, and nothing within miles—with the exception of Hunt's appearance—could distract him from the thousand-year-old spectacle that had outlasted myth, feudal struggles, and impoverishment. He knew no greater aphrodisiac than the history of Athens. The find of the century baiting a man to search for knowledge that could not be acquired in one lifetime.

Rarely had anything but Athena's temple occupied his thoughts. When he wasn't thinking about Athens, he cursed himself for a fool for not being a normal man and choosing a wife. But what kind of woman would live like this?

"Smythe." Baros's voice turned serious.

Spencer turned, following the track of the man's finger, which pointed in the other direction. "If you haven't spotted Hunt or Elgin, I'm not interested."

"*Tha eisai.*"

"English, please. And what could be—"

"People."

People roamed the Acropolis daily. That wasn't surprising. The only two people who concerned him most were the Englishmen he'd been sent to consult and, by all accounts, they were nowhere to be found. Dismissing Baros, he went back to reviewing the map of metopes and friezes he was in the process of drawing, and the damaged pieces of sculpture lying on the ground near his feet. "If it's not Elgin or Hunt, I'm not interested."

"But they are *Ingiliz.*"

He glanced up in spite of himself, his heartbeat quickening. Natives of his homeland? A rare sighting, indeed. "British, you say?"

Baros nodded.

"Where?"

"*Orasi!*" He pointed to the base of a group of stairs where a local man pointed to a portion of the temple, leaning closer as the guides usually did to earn their keep. "There!"

Spencer studied the couple, a peculiar sensation seizing him. Familiarity surrounded this particular English gentleman, dressed in finely cut clothes and sporting an adventurous demeanor. The man obviously had access to amenities few possessed this far from home, a hint that they may have walked in the same circles.

Men like this one came and went, seeking all things Greek, Roman, and Egyptian with an air of defiance few managed. This man, however, held himself differently. He took to the climes as if he'd been born to them.

The woman, too, gave him reason to pause. Dressed rather like her companion in light colors and trousers, instead of skirts, there was something about her very nature that forewarned she was no simpering female to be trifled with. Indeed, she was a vision, a unicorn, the type of woman he hoped to find and feared he wouldn't.

The couple moved to a new vantage point, their direction leading them closer. He stared with appreciation, studying her walk and the motion of her hips, awe taking hold.

Who was this magnificent creature? He had to admit the two of them made a striking pair.

A wicker hat hid a full head of her dark hair, and the flowing ribbon preventing it from flying away, frolicked in the breeze. Glasses sat on the bridge of her nose, masking her eyes in the glinting sunlight, giving her a studious air that he predicted was firmly established by years of book learning. This revelation, at the last, as he focused on her face, gave him pause. She reminded him of someone he'd known long ago, a youthful flower who's love of books led him to taunt her much-too callously.

Baros, apparently tired of Spencer's woolgathering, broke off and approached the pair, starting a conversation. Several moments later, he motioned to Spencer animatedly. "Boss!"

Suddenly eager to oblige, Spencer studied the Englishman as he approached, recognition infiltrating his bones. "Grey!" he shouted. "By Jove! Say it isn't so."

Grey shifted his attention away from the woman at his side. "Kilverstone?"

"It is you," Spencer exclaimed, moving toward his old friend. "What brings you to Athens?" He took him into a brotherly embrace. "How long has it been, old friend?"

"Three eventful years," Grey said smoothly as if time held little relativity.

"I was under the impression you had taken orders."

"Can you imagine?" The laughter the enveloped them swept them immediately back to days spent passing exams and not getting caught sneaking out for a dram. "No, Kilverstone. I left Egypt to report for a different sort of penance."

"Ah." He remembered the solemn event. "Your father's death. Unfortunate, that." He cleared his throat, uneasy for having brought up a conversation Grey certainly did not want to share. "Were you able to see him at the last?"

Grey shook his head. In all the years that Spencer had known him, his friend's one desire had been to make his father proud.

Spencer laid a hand on Grey's shoulder, offering comfort. "I am certain he knew how hard you worked to please him."

"A father would die thinking he'd failed his duty otherwise," Grey said. "At least, that is my hope."

Spencer nodded. Then, realizing belatedly that the others stared on in confusion—especially the remarkably familiar woman at Grey's side, a significant blunder on his part—he set out to rectify the introductions immediately.

"Forgive my poor manners, my lady." He bowed his head with as much of a civilized air as he could manage, covered in dust from head to foot, and after years spent away from London. "I am a fool for not acknowledging your presence before trifling with this old sot."

"The fault is mine," Grey said. "Allow me to introduce Lady Charlotta Grey—formerly Miss Charlotta Walcot—my wife."

"Miss Charlotta . . . Walcot?" The words spewed from his lips before he had time to rein them in. He could remember a time Grey vowed never to marry after—"But I thought . . ." He looked deeply into Lady Grey's eyes, then took a step back. The young whisp of a girl stood before him without any books, the years turning her into an unequaled beauty. "It cannot be." There was no mistaking the likeness, however. "Surely not." He looked to Grey for confirmation. "You did it, didn't you? By Jove. You actually married Little Lottie! But this is magnificent. Very fine, indeed. But what are you doing here, of all places? I thought you had put antiquities behind you. And yet, here you are, with your new wife."

Lady Grey's brown eyes sparked with mirth.

"Forgive this old fool, Lottie," Grey told her. "Don't listen to a word he says."

"And who, pray tell, is this nameless man," she asked grinning, though he had an inkling that she already knew.

Regaining his faculties, Spencer bowed his head to show that years away from civilization had not robbed him of manners. Good fortune had fallen upon Grey. He'd reunited with his long-lost love and grabbed happiness by the bollocks. A hint of jealousy sparked within at the man's luck. "Spencer Wright-Smythe, at your service," he said.

"*The* Baron of Kilverstone?"

He leaned forward, winking. "One and the same, but I prefer Wright-Smythe."

"If I recall, you used to tease me cruelly about my extensive reading," she complained.

"Did I?" From their first meeting, he'd been impressed by the differences between Lottie and other young girls her age. Her ability to memorize specific dates and places had put him to shame. But he also remembered being angry with Grey over his decision to desert Lottie out of respect for their professor, her father, Mr. Walcot. She would not know that, of course, and probably still believed the worst of him after all these years.

"I hated you for it," she admitted, proving his suspicions correct.

"Ah." And with good reason. "Forgive a man his wayward youth."

She smiled then regarded Grey, her gaze settling on him like a silken caress. "All is forgotten . . . as well as forgiven."

"I am a lucky man, Wright-Smythe."

"That is obvious," he said, eager to know how Grey had managed to win back Lottie's love and shackle himself in marriage after so many years spent apart. "And I approve. What brings you both to Athens?"

"A promise made long ago." Grey smiled, his gaze a level-headed beam of contentment. "We are finally taking the Tour."

"An extraordinary adventure that has exceeded my imaginings," Lady Grey said.

Grey himself looked sheepish, his mind most assuredly recalling the promise he'd made Lottie long ago before deserting her without a by your leave, ultimately breaking her heart. The act—one he'd disapproved of—had put Spencer off of love for fear he'd replicate the same choices, given the opportunity. Now, he wasn't so sure. What he would not give to find a woman like Lottie, one willing to leave England and follow his dreams.

Lady Grey met his gaze. "And what brings you here, if I may be so bold?"

"The Acropolis," he said roughly. Being unable to conclude his business with Hunt threatened to keep him from enjoying such a welcome reunion but he did not care. "Forgive my method." He cleared his throat, hoping to turn the conversation to more entertaining themes. "What I mean to say is this is such a welcome surprise." He reached out and shook Grey's hand. "I cannot believe you are standing before me, and married to Little Lottie at that."

It was a joyful announcement, truly. He'd known for years that Grey loved the girl. Oh, she was not her father's young, insatiable, apprentice anymore, but a woman grown. A woman with beauty that radiated inward and outward, intriguing a man's wayward soul. "Where are you staying?"

Grey began to speak then backed off, allowing Lottie to share the details. "We acquired lodging in the heart of Athens."

Which were not what the aristocracy usually inhabited. Unlike the original city structures outlasting the ravages of earthquakes, war, and time, the current, humble city of Athens was built with mud and clay. "The cottages are not the best accommodations, I'll grant you. But, of course, knowing you both as I once have, I wager that is not a deterrent."

"No." The way Lottie looked at Septimus practically screamed that they'd recently wed. His roguish eye could spot besotted lovers anywhere. "That is not why we are here."

Grey's smile reassured him that his gift of perception hadn't waned in his quest to safeguard the Marbles. "It is not."

"I see." But he didn't. Not really. He was nearly thirty without much to show for it. How had Grey and Little Lottie reconnected after years of miscommunication and separation? If Grey could do it . . . Well, couldn't he put aside his rakish ways and find himself a wife? "How long do you anticipate you'll be staying in Athens?"

"Long enough to convince you to accompany us to London."

"London?" Spencer couldn't believe his ears. Grey sounded so self-assured. "I assumed you were headed to Egypt."

"That was to be the last leg of our Tour," Grey said. "But after—"

"The letter." Lottie borrowed her husband, whispering in his ear. At Grey's nod, she said, "I have long desired to go to Egypt, but there is someone I would very much like you to meet before it's too late."

"Too late?" He blinked, looking around as if he'd missed another member of their party. "Is there someone else with you? Someone I have missed?"

"Not here," she said. "In London." She smiled sweetly, but he knew the game Lottie played. The same gestures and traps she'd used in her youth had no hold on him now. Shockingly, she produced a letter. "I have just received word that my cousin, Thenie, is in trouble."

"You remember her," Grey interjected with a frown. "Lottie's uncle, the viscount's eldest daughter."

He groped his memory, only able to recall the viscount. "I cannot say I remember your cousin."

"We grew up together, and I think you might be the one person who can save her."

"Me?" He returned to his drawings, purposefully shutting her out. Rescuing a damsel, he'd never met, was out of the question. He was not a mythical god determined to right a series of wrongs. Besides, the method probably entailed making promises he could not keep. He was not a cit. "The Ottoman need me here. I am verifying Elgin's firman."

Grey produced a locket, opened the outer lid, and handed the bob to Spencer. There, nested within, was a miniature portrait of the most beautiful woman he had ever seen. "Lottie's cousin, Miss Parthenia Steere."

"Is this a good likeness?" he asked before glancing away and inhaling deeply. He'd never considered himself a hero. War had left its indelible mark. Since then, his life had been completely immersed in marble and architecture, an occupation that failed to keep him warm at night, he might add, but felt less threatening. Pacing the Eastern entrance to the temple, he had to wonder, what did he have to lose?

Nothing.

He had no excuses. Hunt avoided him like the plague. Perhaps traveling to England would widen his investigation of the firman Elgin claims the Ottoman gave him. The Marbles were housed in the British Museum. There was little he could do here to prove Elgin was a thief. He'd tried everything and failed thus far.

"A scandal is brewing. If my cousin does not wed soon, my family will be ruined."

Lottie's turmoil jolted him to his marrow. Suddenly, everything made perfect sense. "You knew I was here, Grey." He shook his fist. "That is why you came."

"We've been in Athens for a sennight, but the letter arrived only yesterday. We have been scheming how to save our cousin, afraid we'd never find the answer."

"Until we saw you," she said softly. "You have a good heart, Wright-Smythe. I remember it well. I can think of no better man than you to save my cousin's reputation."

Indeed, he had stayed true to Lottie all these many years, blaming Grey for having deserted her. But this was *his* life, and marriage was a big step. His *good heart* sank into his stomach. He snatched the locket, begrudgingly, and examined the face of Miss Parthenia Steere once more. The artist was talented, talented enough to create an image far from exact. If Miss Steere was half as adventurous as Lottie, however, he'd be a fool not to at least meet her.

"She's in trouble, you say?"

"Yes," Grey said. "Though the time it took the letter to reach us is anybody's guess."

All he had to do was accompany the Greys to London. Would that be so large a sacrifice?

"When do we leave?"

CHAPTER TWO

When your kind eyes looked languishing on mine,
And wreathing arms did soft embraces join,
A doubtful trembling seized me first all o'er,
Then wishes, and a warmth unknown before;
What followed was all ecstasy and trance,
Immortal pleasures round my swimming eyes did dance,
And speechless joys, in whose sweet tumults tost,
I thought my breath and my new being lost.

—*John Dryden*, State of Innocence and Fall of Man: An Opera,
act iii. sc. i.

Mayfair, April 1815

"THEY'RE HERE!" THENIE declared running to the window and
pulling open the sash. Exhilaration flooded her senses, and
several sets of footfalls followed hers. Soon, the front bay window
offered little room for anyone to view the street. "Do you see them,
Mama?"

"Not yet." Even her mother, Lady Mary Steere, could barely control her enthusiasm after practically raising Thenie's cousin, Lottie,
and seeing her off for a honeymoon on the Grand Tour. "Oh, I do

now. I daresay, I do." Mama grabbed her skirts and sashayed to the door. "To the stoop. We must form a welcoming committee, immediately."

Thenie's twin sisters, Augusta and Delphi, two of the most curious eavesdroppers she'd ever met, rushed into the parlor, their faces exhibiting a mix of impatience and delight.

"Can it be true?" Augusta exclaimed with a soft exhale. "Has Lottie finally returned?"

"What do you suppose she brought back from her travels? Gold trinkets? Ancient busts?" Delphi asked.

"Another repulsive mummy?" Augusta wrinkled her nose comically as she and Delphi shared a look of disgust. "I cannot abide decaying, foul-smelling, crypt keepers. They are dreadful and—"

"Yes." Thenie interrupted her sisters' menagerie of complaints. If not tended, they'd grow unpleasantly tiresome. "We are quite aware you do not share Uncle's appreciation for artifacts whether pristine or . . . long since wasted away." She stepped back from the window, a pitty-pat quickening inside her as an enclosed carriage sporting the Walcot crest pulled to a stop in front of the townhouse. Joy leapt inside her. Lord Grey and Lottie were home, at last. Her beloved cousin—more like the twin she'd never had, because they'd grown up together and were the same age—had returned from her honeymoon and the adventure of a lifetime.

Oh, how Thenie had missed her dear cousin's companionship and laughter. Balls, picnics, and rides in Hyde Park had failed to soothe the ache of her absence. Every night for the past six months, Thenie had fought off images of something untoward happening to Lottie in faraway lands, dreading that she'd never be able to confide her deepest, darkest secrets and benefit from her cousin's brilliant advice.

And oh, how she needed Lottie's guidance now.

Shadows loomed all around her.

Augusta had Delphi to confide in, whereas Thenie had always

sought out her cousin when their fathers frittered away time digging up the past. They'd never been apart this long, however. And after taking the long-awaited tour, Lord Grey had promised Lottie when they were young, she could not wait to hear the details of their explorations.

Rushing to the foyer, she nearly ran into Greaves—the aged butler who'd been with the family since her birth, safeguarding their failings. He opened the double doors at the entrance to the townhouse and offered her a purposeful nod, his stoic expression a dreadful thing to behold.

Sunshine spilled in on radiant beams, prisms of light illuminating the black and white marquee floor polished to a dazzling sheen. Daylight and the spring chill air combined splendidly—no rain in sight—an excellent sign that all would be right as long as no one sabotaged the buoyancy of the moment.

Much had happened in her cousin's absence, and to her revolting shame. The people of London prized secrets, gossipmongers daily plotting to depose the wealthy. Matchmaking mamas pushed their young protégés toward eligible bachelors, often at the expense of innocent wallflowers. Especially during the Season when sharpened wits and attending ears absorbed tittle-tattle to quell the boredom. Such was the *ton*.

Thenie silently prayed Lottie's arrival would remedy her woes, casting out the demons that preyed on her sanity. Her dearest cousin's presence would surely provide comfort, a safe haven even as her arrival generated the grandest affair to happen to the family since her cousin's marriage to Septimus, Baron Grey. The couple's surprising reunion, the rekindling of their youthful love and adoration, and their subsequent wedding proved love conquered all.

But could her loving family save her?

Thenie felt privileged to have been a part of Lottie and Grey's journey, however small her role might have been, and she wondered, in retrospect, how altered her cousin would be after fulfilling her childhood dream of traveling the world.

Oh, to face such risky ventures and live to tell the tale!

But that was Lottie's dream, wasn't it? Not hers. It could never be hers. As a viscount's daughter, she was expected to marry well and pave the way for her sisters. Her lot required producing heirs, maintaining a successful household, and earning esteem.

Heaving a sigh, she lowered the hand raised to her eyes to shade them from the sun. She stepped off the stoop, her blood rushing. A flush of happiness threaded its way to her cheeks as the long overdue coach, its rickety wheels and horses' hooves clip clopping along the cobblestones, lumbered to a stop. Seconds ticked by excruciatingly slow, and her anticipation mounted before the driver unceremoniously dismounted and labored to lower the steps.

The first to emerge was Lord Grey, dressed in his customary black and bestowing them with the broadest of smiles. He turned with a flourish and extended his hand to someone seated within.

Lottie. It had to be.

Surrounded by her mother and father, Everard, Viscount Steere, her twin sisters, and several maids and footmen—Thenie finally caught the first glimpse of her extraordinary cousin looking refreshed and so much older and wiser than she remembered.

The hem of Lottie's white gown overlapped the carriage's threshold then covered the stairs, her hat bedecked with saffron-ribbons followed, its wide brim overshadowing her once cream-colored face.

Lottie looked up, sunlight glinting off her glasses, and gave her husband a lovely smile, her joy far-exceeding Thenie's hopes.

Oh, to be loved and cherished in such a way as Lady Lottie Grey.

True to form, the twins disobeyed mama's orders and flocked to Lottie's side, their constant chatter hard to differentiate. Lottie, in a state of apparent amusement, shifted her attention from her husband to the girls, to her expectant family, and faithful servants, all of whom stood at attention, eagerly waiting to be acknowledged.

Then, at last, their eyes met, and Thenie felt the weight she'd been carrying fall away.

"Thenie!" Grey assisted Lottie down the steps. In a flash, everything around them faded into oblivion as she and her cousin shared a long-awaited embrace. "What a wonderful welcome. How good of you all to greet us!"

"How I have missed you so," Thenie exclaimed.

Augusta approached with the prettiest of smiles, hinting that she'd reached the pinnacle of her impatience. "Thenie has been at the window for hours, even though I reminded her that keeping vigil was pure folly. Oh, but now you are here, and you are a beautiful sight and—"

"We are ever so happy you have returned," Delphi finished for her twin. "But what kept you? Were you not expected to arrive several hours ago?"

Lottie joined her gloved hands and smiled, momentarily distracted as her lady's maid, Clara, exited the carriage. She whispered something to Clara, who dipped a curtsy, then scuttled silently up the steps. "I beg your forgiveness, but our delay has surely been for a good cause. You see, we were tasked with providing our friend a short tour of the city."

"What—"

"Friend?" Delphi finished for Augusta.

Thenie was too caught up in the moment to care as Augusta went on. "We should have a ball to celebrate your return."

"Oh, yes!" Delphi somehow managed to contain her excitement. "Please say you will host a ball, Papa."

Before her father answered, the horses whinnied and the equipage alerted them that someone labored to exit the carriage. *How strange.* No one else was expected to arrive. Nonetheless, a man emerged, and the sight of his large hand as he braced the hat on his head and the width of his broad shoulders shifting with the effort, turned Thenie's world upside down.

Oh, he was a marvelous creature! Rugged and raw and robust. As if a statue of Herakles himself had come to life.

His very presence heightened her awareness to the air she breathed, the feel of the breeze on her skin, the sky, and the foundations firmly planted beneath her feet. Her mercenary heart cantered toward the precipice, and she stood motionless while the fellow's lithe and raw movements as he descended the conveyance, his large body monopolizing the doorway, stole her breath.

She sighed incredulously. Oh, but he was handsome!

A noteworthy problem.

Thenie wasn't the sort of woman to swoon at the sight of an adventurer, for that was the only acceptable description she could think of to fit the man. He was tall, sporting fawn shirt and trousers, and knee-high boots. Appropriately dressed like her father and uncle had been when they returned from expeditions to Hadrian's Villa and Egyptian tombs. It was a familiar sight like the morning sun streaming in through laundered curtains, and yet . . . it felt completely unnatural.

She knew why. This man wasn't just any adventurer. He was a relic hunter, the deadliest type of explorer to the female heart. A man who loved and left. The very idea she was attracted to such a one charged her blood, making it run hot and wild like a torrent of flood water. Men like this one drew scholars to the unknown. He was a rare species, a novel breed of man. And her world tilted on axis as Herakles, in human form, approached Grey, every motion he made stealing her breath.

Expectation hitched in her belly.

He is extraordinary, and my inability to do more than stand and stare makes me appear reckless. Am I not already in a fix?

Grey towered over her by a head. But this scoundrel rose five inches taller than Grey, forcing her head back as she studied the brim of his hat, and the way it shaded his calm and collected, impassive blue eyes.

For the entirety of her life, she had schooled herself to want more than what her father and uncle lusted after—artifacts, fame, knowledge—the dirt and mud and dust nearly choking out their family life. To compensate, she had set her cap for civilization, balls, lace, silk, delicate china, tea parties and Society, not the abandonment mama was forced to endure.

And yet, Mama—in all her solitude and refinement—proved to be one of the happiest, most settled women she knew, a woman strengthened by purpose, art, and history.

Lost in her thoughts, she failed to notice the greetings diminished. She blinked, batting away the spell the stranger had woven over her as Lottie adjusted the brim of her glasses and said, "Good heavens! I beg, forgive my incivility. We have not returned empty handed, as you can already see, for we discovered our friend in Athens." She lifted her hand and motioned the outsider forward. "Allow me to present our inventive companion." She directed the man to Thenie's parents first. "Lord and Lady Steere—my aunt and uncle—and my cousins, Miss Steere, and Misses Augusta and Delphi . . ." Curtsies and bows were traded. "I present to you, Mr. Spencer Wright-Smythe."

The stranger's impenetrable gaze settled on Thenie, his advantage in size declaring him far superior and intellectual than the men she was accustomed to dealing with. It was unfair to embrace such prejudice or withhold a penchant for it, and yet she clung to his handsome qualities like never before. His searching eyes probed her soul, delighting her consciousness. It was as if she knew him. That she'd always known him. That she'd never spent a single moment in time without this man by her side. His handsome face, his rugged and strong jawline, straight nose, and soul-piercing eyes prevented her from forming words.

"Thenie?"

She blinked as the sound of her name sucked her back into reality, making her shockingly aware that she'd been caught staring.

"Are you unwell?" Lottie grasped her forearm. "I have never seen you in such a state. Did you not hear me introduce our friend?"

"Forgive my ghastly manners." She shook her head, stamping out her embarrassment as her mother and sisters curtsied to the gentleman. "The thrill of seeing both of you again has left me . . . speechless."

"Of course," Lottie said with a smile. "That is perfectly understandable."

She looked past her cousin, inviting the stranger into her realm. Then, she dropped a curtsy, hardly able to form words. "How do you do?"

He caught her hand and raised it to his lips, his touch firm and persuasive as time lost all relevance and their gazes locked. "The pleasure is mine."

Saints be praised! What is happening to me?

He bowed his head, his smile warm and inviting. "I have heard a lot about you, Miss Steere."

She shot a look at Lottie, her confusion complete. How and when had they discussed her? And what had been said?

"Is something wrong?" Lottie embraced her impulsively. "I thought you would be happy to see us." *Us?* The rogue's gaze branded her, filling her with a strange tingling heat that inhabited her belly with a resourcefulness beyond measure. The feeling was altogether peculiar, especially since she despised the roles relic hunters played.

"I am overjoyed to see you, of course," she insisted nervously. Lottie abandoned her for Grey and Augusta and Delphi, leaving her alone with the handsome outsider. But no one had ever scrambled her faculties as this man did, and words failed her, yet again.

"Cat got your tongue?"

She tsked at his rudeness. "Unlikely, sir."

"How so?"

"Well . . . first, I would have to inform you that I do not have a cat."

"No cats?" he asked. "May I ask, why not?"

25

"You may. I live in the city and do not need a lap warmer."

"What a shame." He looked her over, the anticipation of what he'd say next almost unbearable. "I do."

"Sir." His teasing frazzled her nerves, heightening her irritation. "Vulgarity may be celebrated on foreign soil, but in Britain, manners and decorum must always be in famous supply."

"Are you not aware?" His brow danced, lifting the lock of hair that escaped from the brim of his hat. "I *am* British." That was debatable. The color of his skin provided him a Grecian look that contradicted any English upbringing, and his manner . . . "But if I have offended you, that was not my intention. Please excuse my less than exemplar behavior."

Inferior, he was not. *Drat!* She might possibly be able to overlook a man's bad conduct, but not this one's handsome attributes. How fine he looked, standing there in his weathered splendor. *Oof!* She abhorred how his very presence manipulated her thoughts. And how he did so by doing nothing at all . . . it was mystifying.

"Y-You do not look the part," she said, trying to figure out how to reject his attention without offending her cousins. The threat of scandal was ever present to young women. She couldn't afford to encourage any man lest she end up married to him. Certainly, not after Boothe discredited her at Mrs. Beaumont's ball. Speaking rhetorically about a kiss had backfired on both of them, because no one survived whispers of impropriety. The *ton* was a cruel master. "In London, there are expectations."

"Which I endeavor to meet."

Good God, she was in genuine trouble. *The wrong of it!* Permitting this scoundrel to believe flattery and flirtation overruled good sense. Rumormongers salivated for such a sight. Spiteful lies were yesterday's news, of course—damn his eyes—hurtful, and particularly inopportune. Even Lottie had had to hire someone to investigate who was blackmailing her father before his flawless reputation was ruined.

He lowered his head slightly then placed her hand over the crook of his arm to escort her indoors. "If you will allow me, of course."

"You are too forward by half," she said with Lottie in her sights. Could her cousin not see her distress? The threat of mortification made her long for a quick death. And a speedy demise was exactly what her innocence experienced as Grey's friend slackened his grip and searched her soul with an earnestness that touched her deeply. "Release me. Please."

"Did you know that in Rome, cats are independent creatures. In Greece, they are considered clever and bewitching." His husky tone infiltrated the fine cloth of her gown, tautening the strings buttressing her heart. Her bosom heaved with anticipation and, darn her, a longing to know more of him.

"What does any of that have to do with me?"

"I am trying to decide if you are wild or domesticated, Miss Steere."

Curiosity was a dangerous thing. "Care killed the cat."

His throaty laughter irritated her more than words could say.

Why? She'd changed in her cousin's absence, interpretations of her existence shifting—her ambitions too. As much as she longed for High Society, rank and riches, caring not for affections of the heart, the love she'd witnessed between her cousin and Grey pierced her depths.

She wanted the same for herself and her sisters, but how would she know? Would that awareness come in a look, a man's words, his touch . . . a kiss?

Prearranged marriages unified families and properties, deepening pockets and thickening alliances. These were loveless couplings—illusionary. And the thought of being commonplace, stuck in an arrangement that benefited no one, sickened her. Nevertheless, she had a duty to perform. She was the eldest daughter of a viscount destined to wed before her sisters. Espousing out of order simply wasn't done. And since Augusta and Delphi had come of age, sharing their hopes and dreams and filling Thenie with imaginings for their foreseeable futures, the pressure weighing on her shoulders grew more intense.

Inversely, if she waited to marry for love, all sorts of chaos would ensue. For instance, what if the right man never came along and she'd waited for nothing? What if Augusta and Delphi suffered because Thenie refused to wed, losing the loves of their lives in the process?

She couldn't allow that to happen. Lottie had come home. Her cousin, in all her wisdom, would know what to do, where to turn. She had a talent for calming the bees in Thenie's bonnet.

"You have a sharp wit."

"This," she said, pointing to their interlocked arms, "isn't done." Her agitation for the man increased by the minute. "You do not know me at all, Mr.—"

"Wright-Smythe, at your service."

"Mr. Wright-Smythe, this *is* my cousin's day and your forward behavior has complicated it."

"Complications have merit." He leaned close, his breath a whisper away. "I hear they often lead to wonderful discoveries."

She agreed in part, but only because his presence and his advances filled her with a strange longing. The discovery that she enjoyed it went against her better judgment. "That may be true in Athens but here, complications lead to scandal and scandal, sadly, to ostracism."

"Isolation can be endured with the right person." He appeared thoughtful as the procession began to move. "But I see you are single-minded." He seized the knot of his cravat, giving her the impression that he longed to rip it off. She imagined him standing by Athenian ruins, the sun bathing his face, the top of his collar unlaced with a hint of musculature visible beneath. *Shocking!* His laughter made her wonder if he'd read her thoughts. "I must commend, Lady Grey. She assured me you would be quite diverting."

Practical. *I am practical.*

She had to be.

"If it is entertainment you seek, I recommend you look elsewhere." Places like the Lyon's Den, with its strategic location in Whitehall, its rich clientele and vetted employees, provided the type of satisfaction a feral man like Wright-Smythe would no doubt find diverting. "Perhaps Grey can assist you."

"Grey brought me *here*." He studied her beneath the brim of his hat. His eyes were elusive and darkened by shadows. "And if I may be so bold, I would like to offer that I sense you are hiding spirited inclinations."

"Oof!" Her gasp drew attention. To quickly cover her gaffe, she pretended to laugh, which seemed to appease Mama momentarily. "How dare you," she spat. "You know nothing about me, nothing at all. You have made it blatantly clear that we are from two vastly different worlds. Why, I cannot imagine us being more dissimilar."

"Perhaps we are not so unalike, you and I, that you would refuse to allow me to escort you indoors." He winked, his charming grin hard to resist. "Before you tire of our banter and seek to disorient me."

She didn't realize her mouth had fallen open until he gently nudged her chin closed. As she bristled from the contact, feeling it trace a path all the way to her toes, a triumphant smile transformed his face. Blood rushed through her veins, heat kindling every fiber of her being.

The fool thought he'd won her over. *Hadn't he?*

She tore her gaze away, desperate to ignore the gloating man as they locked arms and he chaperoned her inside. There, Greaves supervised, and footmen retrieved their outer garments. Mama requested for tea to be sent to the parlor. The group followed, her sisters chatting away, before Papa asked for everyone's attention. A hush fell in the vestibule, one that seemed to drone on excessively long, increasing the tension mounting inside Thenie as her father approached the man standing by her side.

"Grey tells me you have been investigating the Marbles. How did you—"

"Meet?" the newcomer finished for Papa with polished charm.

Grey joined them, his winsome smile infectious. "Your daughter and I were being given a tour of the Acropolis by our guide in Athens when the man spotted Kil—" he cleared his throat as if he'd been about to disclose something else before changing track "—Wright-Smythe making some sketches."

Thenie's impression of Wright-Smythe took a jolt. "You are an artist?"

"Some think so," he admitted humbly.

"A fine artist," Lottie interjected. "Exquisite renderings. If only you had seen them, Thenie. The Marbles." She clapped her hands together as if enthralled by the memory. "You simply had to be there. The temple, dedicated to the goddess Athena still stands in colossal wonderment, its once white marble aged to a sepia hue. Porticos, chambers, friezes and reliefs are magnificent to behold, each one hiding a story or hidden meaning. And though I once did, I do not fault Lord Elgin for absconding with the Marbles and desiring to preserve their beauty. Nevertheless—"

"Do not encourage her, Lottie," Papa said. "The Marbles are not the stuff for unmarried females."

"So, you have seen them, my lord?"

"I have, Wright-Smythe, though not in their natural setting. My brother and I have studied them in the British Museum where Elgin stores them. I know that the temple they were taken from has a long history of being a Byzantine church, a Roman Catholic cathedral, as well as a mosque. And, after the center of it was destroyed, Venetians smashed priceless sculptures while attempting to carry them off." Papa inhaled deeply, sadness lingering on his face. "A shame, by all accounts. The artistry and craftsmanship cannot be comprehended unless witnessed in person. Not in pieces. So, yes. If you are wondering what I think about Elgin's decision to transport the Marbles to England, I would have to say that I question his method of dividing the relics from their birthplace."

Grey said, "I was under the impression that the Ottomans insist the artifacts were removed without a firman."

"Elgin insists he procured one. Though the damn fool has yet to produce it, putting the museum in the crosshairs." Papa lit a cigar. "Do you know Elgin, Wright-Smythe?"

"I have not—as yet—had the pleasure of making his acquaintance. Nevertheless, it is my personal understanding that he is an arguable fellow."

Thenie couldn't believe that Wright-Smythe offered his opinion, of a man he'd never met, so freely. And in front of her father, no less. Papa had not gained a renowned reputation for bartering antiquities legally from other countries for nothing, and she valued his point of view greatly. Her uncle's too. Hadn't he spent years digging at Hadrian's Villa before discovering Lord Lansdowne's Herakles and elsewhere, by default earning the right to voice his opinions?

"You say," Thenie began, "that Lord Elgin is an arguable fellow, and yet, you have never met him."

"I think our friend objects to Elgin's practice of pillaging ruins for his own gain," Grey said.

Delphi, surprising them all by sitting still for so long, could do so no longer. "But isn't that the reason my uncle goes to Egypt?"

Lottie gasped. "Delphi. How can you even suggest that my father is duplicitous in illegal proceedings? You have seen how diligent he has been with the Rosetta Stone."

Delphi tried to explain. "I would—-"

"Never!" Augusta raged. "How can you—"

"Even suggest such a thing?" Delphi finished for her.

"One's view of robbery depends on which side one is on." Sage wisdom and an intriguing surprise coming from Wright-Smythe.

Thenie had never once given much thought to the places relics had been acquired, except for the extraordinary history that could be, and should be, shared with the masses.

Further discussion on the subject ended when tea arrived, the silver service gleaming in the window light, and the pungent aroma—bitter and spice—filling the room. China clattered, the sound filling the silence, annoying Thenie's already frazzled nerves.

Her mother, ever the perfect hostess, served. Refreshments were consumed, time passing in a blur. Thenie's desperation mounted. Still, she soaked in every nuance and historical reference to the Marbles, mesmerized by Wright-Smythe's passion for them. Had he taken molds of the sculptures? Touched them with his strong hands?

Conversation went on into the night. They discussed the history of the Acropolis, known to ancient Greeks as Cecropia after the mythical serpent-man who founded Athens and became its first king. The site comprised of the Temple of Athena, and ancient theaters and legends, like the famous outcrop where Ares was tried for the murder of Poseidon's son. Each topic heightened her appreciation for Wright-Smythe and his devotion to Athens, filling her with a mushrooming desire to find a way to see the Marbles for herself.

But that was an impossible hope, wasn't it?

"Marbles are not the stuff for unmarried females."

CHAPTER THREE

*Around Town, you'll find rakes and debauchees are your men of
pleasure; thoughtless atheists, and illiterate drunkards, call
themselves free thinkers; and gamesters, banterers, biters, swearers,
and twenty new-born insects more, are, in their several species, the
modern men of wit. Hence it is, that a man who has been out of town
but one half-year, has lost the language, and must have some friend to
stand by him, and keep him in countenance for talking common
sense. But let a woman mention a kiss and virtue, once regaled,
is gone.*

—The Morning Post

T HERE WERE PERKS to delving into the field of antiquities. Indiffer-
ence to the *beau monde*. Travel to ancient cities, indulging in
primitive cultures, making historic finds, and gaining membership into
the small conclave of like-minded adventurers. Physical labor sum-
moned the fearless. The antiquities market enticed financiers, the
prospect of making the discovery of a lifetime ever balanced on a roll
of the dice. Much, for instance, like speculating on a game of chance in
gambling hells, risking legacies, and using them as collateral in
Whitehall at the Lyon's Den.

The Grey's had discussed the black widow, Mrs. Bessie Dove-
Lyon, wife of the late Colonel Sandstrom Lyon, informing him she

was a woman who took mourning her husband to a new level in a problematic trade. Kind words had been shared about Dove-Lyon, providing information few had on the woman—her acerbic wit and motherly concern for her *little wrens* earning respect from all quarters. And after Spencer's conversation with the Greys about coming to Thenie's rescue, he'd set aside any and all inclinations of seeking the widow's matchmaking skills while in Town.

But never let it be said that a man didn't know when to take advantage of opportunities. He hadn't become one of the richest explorers to date without risking one or two wagers. Few were aware of his monetary success, and he preferred to keep the intimate details of his life just that—private. What wasn't a secret, though he preferred not to use his title, is that he'd been granted a peerage for services rendered during the war. Because of his elevated status, he humbled himself next to men like Lord Lansdowne, Sir Sloane, Lord Granville, Grey, and others, in particular—The Honorable Mr. Bertrand Walcot.

His former professor and confidant had earned his utmost respect in the classroom and the field, teaching him everything there was to know about excavation and preservation. Which made his encounter with the Greys at the Athenian temple, fortuitous.

As it happened, he'd been trapped in a cycle of work and needed the company of old friends, jumping at the chance for a change in scenery after coming to terms with the reason they had sought him out. Joining the Greys made for a happy occurrence combined with business that profited him greatly. Plans to travel to London had already been in the works, making the timing of his encounter with Lottie and Grey most convenient.

Primary on his schedule whilst back in the kingdom was to ensure the firman for Lord Elgin's Marbles had been filed with the British import office. According to the Ottomans, who did not have a firman in hand, Elgin's word as a gentleman had come under intense scrutiny. Therefore, to stave off a war, he'd agreed to look into the situation more thoroughly.

Imagine his surprise—after viewing the locket portrait—that he found himself smitten with Miss Parthenia Steere. Puzzling affair, to say the least. Even though he'd come to assist Miss Steere, she rebuked him at every turn.

Suffice it to say, he wasn't accustomed to being rebuffed. Granted, a man fortunate enough to secure new money seldom found acceptance by members of the *ton*. And while he'd been created a baron with a massive Hall, estate, and tenants, he'd tried to make more of his life than living by the system Society ruled far superior to laboring folk. Tenants depended on the living he provided in Kilverstone—a matter of extreme importance to him and the solicitors he employed. His word was his bond. Whether his revenue was inherited or self-made, he fashioned decency and compassion for those under his employ.

Threadneedle Street allowed him certain pleasures, in particular his fondness for antiquities. A conundrum which prohibited familial relationships, given his lifestyle. It was too much to ask of a woman, to have her turn her back on wealth and status and live with dust and depravity. Nevertheless, Lottie had done it. And the Greys had suggested Thenie fit the mold. That she would make a perfect wife. And after meeting Little Lottie's cousin, the spark between them was electrifying and real and gave him hope that he could marry and continue the work that fulfilled his spirit.

Thenie's wit and ingenuity astounded him on so many levels. Outward appearances meant everything on this island, but a life abroad demanded more. Goodwill and constancy. Here, she excelled. She was the epitome of gentle breeding, and the gleam in her eyes promised a brashness that might very well save her life.

Eager to explore the possibilities, to test her mind, her character, her loyalty, he braced himself for a challenge. Simply put, she, like every other wallflower, would have to be persuaded . . . awakened like a bud swelling in sunlight.

Indeed, he longed to see her hair tumble down around her shoulders, to thread his fingers through the blonde strands. The coiled tresses enhanced her high cheekbones and impressionistic brows. Her suspicious stare challenged him at every turn, snubbing him with a pert nose and bewitching eyes just as blatantly as the friezes on the temple who dared him to understand their purpose.

Antoninus Liberalis shaped myths in the 2nd Century about goddesses like Miss Steere. According to Liberalis, Hera transformed Galinthias into a cat because she'd thwarted the murder of Alcmene and Heracles. What was it Thenie had said about cats?

"Care killed the cat."

Dangers awaited more than cats in Athens, Rome, and Egypt. Times abroad were hard and lonely and women of quality in the archeological sphere were rare and greatly treasured, and likewise sought out for financial or diplomatic gain.

If he could win Thenie's heart, she would need a determined edge and a firm countenance to survive perilous climes. Thankfully, she'd proven herself once over by gracefully welcoming her cousins with an easy smile. What he wouldn't give to be similarly admired. But it was clear, for now, he would have to play his part as her pride and prejudices kept them apart.

They'd only just met. True. But was this Lord Boothe an obstacle to his pursuit of Thenie? According to the Grey's, the young baron had courted her for months. Had an agreement between them been reached? And was that the reason Boothe had overreacted at Mrs. Beaumont's ball?

He flexed his hands, disappointment a familiar feeling but hardly devastating. He would have to charm his way into her good graces. Her younger sisters were not immune. They bat their lashes and stared at him in wide-eyed wonder whenever they thought he wasn't looking.

Lady Steere's voice quieted the conversation. "We have planned a soiree in your honor, Charlotta."

The twins giggled, sharing something humorous between themselves that no one else could hear.

"I have not forgotten how fond you are of balls."

Lottie's voice was warm and genuine, which added to his confusion because he distinctly recalled her telling him she detested attending balls. "How good of you to have gone to so much trouble, for me. We'd be delighted to take part, only if we are to be surrounded by friends,"—she looked at Spencer—"both new, and old. Though I fear, Aunt, you have gone to too much trouble on our account."

"No trouble at all, I assure you. We would be happy for Mr. Wright-Smythe to join us." Thenie looked as if she was about to object before her mother cut her off. "Your presence will bring enjoyment to one, and all, I am sure."

Spencer bowed his head, holding back a grin. "Then, I gladly accept your invitation."

"Mr. Wright-Smythe is merely being polite, Mama," Thenie said. "I am sure he requires more time to familiarize himself with Society."

"A gentleman never forgets," Papa said sternly. "Isn't that so, Grey?"

"Correct." Grey cleared his throat. "Little Lottie?"

"Mr. Wright-Smythe is well-mannered and good." Lottie smiled. "And your concern for him, Thenie, is all that is decent, a testament to your good nature. Perchance, would you be willing to help acclimate our friend to London?"

Brava, Little Lottie. A trap neatly sprung.

"It *has* been an age since I have been in England," he said. "Three years, in fact. How could I refuse such a generous offer?"

"Perhaps you should." Thenie's directness shocked him. "Society isn't kind, Mr. Wright-Smythe. How can I possibly relieve you of the weight of unnecessary anxiety?"

"With kindness." Lord Steere quirked his brow. "Opportunities to gather at social events are rare in a foreign country, my dear. What would you have the man do?"

Grey offered Spencer a nod of encouragement. "Wright-Smythe is not without civility." He motioned his hands to everyone present. "We are all examples of such a living."

"In my opinion, no man should be defined by what he does, but by what he is."

"And what kind of man are you, Mr. Wright-Smythe?" Thenie's question echoed in the stillness.

"By all accounts, I suspect Wright-Smythe is a man who has rescued relics and endured arid climates," Lord Steere said. "There is a commitment to human excellence required in that service."

Steere's support meant a great deal to him, and the viscount's collection was well documented. Because of his contributions, London was quickly becoming the center for timeless artifacts. One needn't go farther than the atrium to see that the viscount's discoveries added brilliance to collections from Hamilton, Sloane, and Lansdowne.

"Storing and exhibiting relics for the masses is a worthy cause," Lady Steere said. "The kingdom has amassed an impressive assortment thanks to my husband and his brother."

"And men like Mr. Wright-Smythe," Lottie said.

"The Honorable Bertrand Walcot." The butler's announcement of a new caller brought the conversation to a halt.

Here, Spencer witnessed the youthful essence of Little Lottie once more as she bolted to her feet. "Papa!"

Walcot opened his arms, enveloping his daughter in his embrace. He shot Grey a smile, filling Spencer with envy. He had always desired children. "Thank you for bringing my daughter back to me." He leaned toward Grey, who whispered something in his ear. "What's that, you say? Wright-Smythe? Here? Where?" He searched the room, his eyes narrowing on each soul. "Wright-Smythe? Is that you?"

Walcot abandoned his daughter's side and scampered closer, his slower gait a pox on the passage of time.

"I am here, sir." Spencer moved toward the man who'd filled his head with notions of distant lands and untold wealth. "In the flesh."

"Why,"—he glared up at him—"I thought . . . Hallelujah! It is you!" He reached for Spencer's hand. "You scamp. I thought you'd never leave Athens! Even a barony—"

"Wouldn't tempt me," he said, cutting the man off before he let the level of his nobility slip.

"But what brings you to my brother's home?" Glancing around the room in confusion, Walcot grinned, his senses rallying. "Let me guess. Lottie and Grey?"

"Yes," he said. "Among other things."

"Such as," Thenie asked, her perfect brows perched above her piercing stare.

Now was the time for honesty. "I have come home to find a wife."

Thenie's rosy lips formed an O, making him ponder their softness, their taste, supposing she would ever let him get close enough to steal a kiss. Something, he assumed, would never happen given the scandal associated with her name. Still, he dared not move. Something intangible hid in the depths of her soul, a hint of desperation and determination—especially defiance.

Would she ever accept him?

"Actually," Lottie admitted, "I invited Mr. Wright-Smythe to London to spend the Season with us for that very reason."

"The *entire* Season?" He had the sneaking suspicion Lottie's confession frustrated Thenie.

"However long it takes, Miss Steere," he admitted.

Lottie patted Thenie's arm and smiled. "I am confident Wright-Smythe will find the perfect bride. Extremely confident."

"I have lost my daughter over marriage. I do not recommend it."

"You will never lose me, Papa," Lottie proclaimed.

Walcot grunted then changed the subject. "And, just like that, you and Grey are thick as thieves again." The professor counted his fingers. "How long has it been?"

"Three years." Grey offered. "I applaud Athens for sustaining my friend's attention this long."

"You have been in Athens for three years?" Thenie asked.

At last, a topic he could fully engage her in. "It is a fascinating area to dig but, sadly, the local inhabitants believe women are a distraction."

"I heartily agree," Walcot said, erupting into laughter. "Apologies to my daughter, but in my experience, a beautiful woman abolishes everything else. In fact, when I traveled to Hadrian's Villa, my—"

"Papa!" Lottie exclaimed, mortified.

Spencer didn't understand their heated exchange, so he said, "I never thought that you, of all people, professor, would believe in such nonsense."

"Thinking on it now, and after taking the Tour, I imagined my daughter would understand things are not done there, the way we practice them on the British Isles."

"Women are not allowed to unearth treasures in foreign lands?" Thenie asked. "Why, that is just as restricting as not being able to go out alone or stroll down certain streets in London."

"Customs are different everywhere," Lord Steere said.

Thenie harrumphed. "Different? Here, ladies are sold in the marriage mart for monetary gain. Mergers chiefly benefiting men, I must add. Moreover, if women find themselves unhappily wed and wish to be freed from their vows, their children are taken and held hostage from them forever. How is that any different?"

"Parthenia!" Lady Steere snapped. *"'Beware you do not lose the substance by grasping at the shadow.'"*

"Aesop!" Augusta and Delphi brooded, depositing themselves on the settee like disconsolate children.

"I think it is clear that *'If you allow men to use you for your own purposes, they will use you for theirs,'*" Thenie replied.

Curse the female mind! What the devil was going on?

Surprised by Thenie's cynicism, Spencer cleared his throat. Arguing about the inferiority of one's status never changed a thing. "Pardon my intrusion. But I am curious about one thing, professor. What is your opinion of Lord Elgin's Marbles?"

Walcot appeared relieved in the change of topic. "You have met them in their natural wonder. I am sure you are probably a better judge of their superior artistry than I. But, yes, I have seen them. The metopes and friezes transported to London are stored in the museum, and I must say they are an exhilarating sight." He paused, puffing on his pipe and creating a whirl of smoke that churned about his face. "To the select, I must add."

"Select?" Lottie asked.

"Meaning," Thenie glumly said. "They are off-limits to the opposite sex."

"Parthenia!" Lady Steere seemed to have reached her limit. "Take care."

The girls shrieked, appalled. "Thenie!"

Thenie's novel notions were applaudable, making him wonder if she disputed the strictness surrounding the Marbles because *she* actually desired to see them.

Was this something he could arrange?

CHAPTER FOUR

He will never have her: for would you believe it, though a Corinthian has wit, good sense, fortune, and his very being depends on her, the termagant for whom he sighs, is in love with a fellow, who stares in the glass all the time he is with her. He pleases himself with vain imagination, supposing that with the language of his eyes, he shall conquer her, though her eyes are intent upon one who looks from her; which is ordinary with the sex. It is certainly a mistake in the ancients. Love is blind, for he is a little thief that squints. Ask Mrs. Beaumont, confidante or spy, and she will tell you the same could be said for Lord B, that the whole is a game of cross purposes. The lover is generally pursuing one who is in pursuit of another. Observe, and you'll find, a woman makes no stay on him they say she is to marry, but rests two seconds of a minute on he who neither looks nor thinks on her.

—The Morning Post

A S THE NIGHTS passed, Thenie's concerns mounted. Her life had taken a new direction, one far different than the one she had ever expected. Had it been that long ago when she had adored balls, the sights, smells, and sounds of couples dancing and laughing? Friendships between strangers blossoming? Nothing had enthralled her more than skipping and sashaying the Season away with gallant

42

partners, the flirtation and frenzy of the crush raising her spirits to dizzying heights. Every opportunity to take part in seasonal soirees had brought expectancy to her breast. Hadn't she said as much to those in her close circle many times over, especially her sister, Delphi?

Saints preserve her, but her life was much altered now. And tonight, another ball threatened her closely monitored world.

Truth be told, Mama had outdone herself with a beautiful assortment of the choicest hot house flowers and glorious grandeur, with nods to antiquity, of course, and a profusion of potted plants. The dance floor was chalked with musicians and young girls with clappers from the Egyptian kingdom, whose long filmy gowns and gestures of grace and elegance fluidly decorated the space. Every aspect of the townhouse held indefatigable attention to detail that left Thenie with a bitter and lasting fear that another group of flibbertigibbets would ruin it all.

How long before she was no longer welcome in Society? Before gossip destroyed her sisters and arranged marriages were their only option, if anyone would have them by then?

Oh, God. I've been foolish . . . selfish.

Nevertheless, she must put that behind her now. She had obligations. She was expected to attend this ball to celebrate her beloved cousins' return, no matter the rumors. Lottie was like a sister as dear as Augusta and Delphi had ever been, having grown up together in the absence of Lottie's mother, and a father who journeyed abroad, spending months in the field without them ever knowing if either Papa or their uncle would return.

Lottie's contagious laughter nearby infiltrated Thenie's thoughts, bringing a smile to her face. How magnificent it was to have her cousin home. The joy strumming through Thenie's heart came to an abrupt halt, however, when her gaze locked onto Wright-Smythe's from across the room.

Grey's friend was the last man she wanted to give her undivided attention to, even if the thought sent a swift thrill clean through to her bones. She didn't need complications—now, here, ever—before her reputation was forever ruined by eavesdroppers and gossipmongers. Turning away, she sipped at her champagne, the only possible way to endure the evening. How long she stood, listening and stewing over her travails, in abject misery, she couldn't be sure. The list of her errors was long, the agony sure to haunt her sisters lasting a lifetime.

A voice broke into her thoughts. "May I have the pleasure of this dance?"

Choking on her champagne, she spun around to find herself face to face with Wright-Smythe. How had he reached her so quickly? Seconds swelled to a minute then another, growing more intense as Thenie realized she was expected to speak. Several elderly women looked on, refereeing her behavior.

There was only one answer she could give him without making a scene. She dipped a curtsy. "You may."

Wright-Smythe took the glass from her hand and set it on a passing footman's tray. "I have been looking forward to this moment all night."

Tensing, she focused on his large, strong hands, trying in vain to ignore the heat penetrating her gloves as he led her to the center of the dance floor. There, she had to wonder what was taking place within her. She had never responded to Boothe in this way—her heartbeat quickening, her chest constricting, the very depth of her soul teased with the pleasure of what might transpire between them.

Why?

Her gaze strayed from his hands to his broad shoulders then to his expressive eyes. His touch, his nearness, had a startling effect on her person. It was shocking, really—no delightful, glorious, overloading her senses with all kinds of feminine nonsense. The sheer power his masculinity afforded her, helped to stave off the stares of envious females in the room, and the barely concealed snarls of conniving mamas.

But wasn't that the purpose of a ball? To be seen. To assemble. To be judged and lifted from obscurity to renown, achieving financial security and the assurances of a better life.

That was not the future she desired for herself or her sisters without love.

Partners exchanged, and she found herself standing in front of Boothe, his sour demeanor weighing heavy on her heart. She'd imagined him to be a good man, incapable of sullying a woman's reputation, especially in public. She'd been wrong, and her fleeting shame as to why *she'd* rejected *him* grieved her deeply as Spencer traded places with Boothe then twirled her back into place. Her heart pounded, the sound deafening, drowning out Gow's band, if one believed that possible. She smiled past the pain, disheartened by the choices she'd made. By pondering a kiss, she had somehow blackened a good man's heart, and he, in turn, had tried to destroy her.

"How does it feel to dance with a wildling?" Wright-Smythe asked.

Oof! "You are a good dancer. If I did not know any better, I would think your years in Athens were not all spent at the Acropolis."

He passed, his breath warming her neck as he drew her close. "I am only repeating what I've heard making the rounds about the room."

"Wildness has its virtues. But, I beg, do not boast of it. Most, here, will not find your observations amusing." He swept her across the dance floor, his movements perfection and in total contrast to everything she knew about this rugged man. "Or proper. We hardly know each other, and you are most forward by half."

"I adore your quick mind." He laughed softly, the sound a pleasant symphony to her ears. "But I am a man of truth. When I say something, I mean it."

"You intend to compare yourself to men I have known all my life, when I have hardly known you nearly a week?"

Wright-Smythe produced that charming grin that set her heart aflutter, and the flash of white teeth between his attractive mouth proved him dauntless and disciplined and difficult to resist. She fought hopelessly to tear her gaze away.

"What is a day or a week?" He winked. "What can be gleaned in a moment, an hour?"

"You think yourself a poet." Or had she had too much champagne?

"I confess to not being born with Byron's talent. In the trenches, however, a man learns to distinguish treasure from twaddle."

She blinked. "Treasure from—"

"It's a talent, I assure you."

They circled the floor in awkward silence. As much as she wanted to escape what his touch was doing to her, no one walked away from the dance without stirring speculation. Scorn and sympathy were the last things she required.

She searched his face. "I have never met a more tenacious man."

"Tenacious? Is that what you think of me?"

"You are determined, sir."

"I know who I am. I also value time." He quirked his brow, the effect enhancing his good looks. "That's the difference."

"And who are you . . . exactly?" she asked, unable to mask her curiosity as they circled each other.

"The man destined to tame you."

Her legs threatened to give way. Had she had too much champagne? She looked away to see if anyone had overheard his ridiculous boast. *Good heavens, my sisters are doomed.* "I am not a creature to be tamed."

"No." He grinned. "You should be treasured. As I said, I know the difference between treasure and twaddle."

"I still do not understand."

"Strength." Their gazes held. "You are a strong woman, Miss Steere. Power emanates from your eyes, and it is fascinating to behold.

A man does not recover from such a woman."

A shiver of delight shot through her. She fought to calm her dizzying mind, unable to stop herself from asking, "What kind of strength?"

The steps to the dance parted them before they came together again. "Beneath your polite veneer lurks a passionate, headstrong, curious woman longing to explore the world and all that inhabits it." His breath was warm and inviting as he drew her toward him, making her long for the intimacy, for his touch, his kiss. "Indeed, you are like Athena, the virginal goddess of war, an enigma, beautiful and alluring, and deadly."

Unable to form words, she realized the irony. *The cat has caught my tongue.*

The music stopped.

He winked then released her hands, bowing before her. She mourned the slow, earth-shattering loss of his tenderness. "Thank you for the dance. I found it . . . enlightening."

He walked away as Lottie gently clutched her hand, the part of her that still tingled. "Thenie, are you unwell?"

"I am . . . quite well, cousin," she said trying to quell the beat of her heart. "Thank you. In fact, I am enjoying myself immensely. But I wonder, what gives you the impression that I am unwell?"

Lottie's brow crooked, troubling the asymmetrical shape of her face. "I saw you dancing with Wright-Smythe and I thought—"

"Yes," she finished for her on a sigh. "We danced."

Lottie adjusted the rim of her glasses. "You are flushed and I wanted to make sure that you were not ill. Or that my friend has not done something untoward. He has been away from civilization a very long time as you pointed out. If he has done something to offend you—"

"Do not worry." She laughed, the jovial expression she hoped to present sounding unnatural. A tell Lottie would not likely miss. "I am quite well."

But she wasn't, and no doubt Lottie knew it.

She shivered. Wright-Smythe had turned her entire world upside down and inside out, and her ambitions to embers. "It is the heat, surely," she insisted.

"Since the two of you just danced, I simply must ask. What do you think of him?"

Crying foul served to only increase her cousin's fascination with what had occurred between them. "He is rugged—"

"Ly handsome." Candlelight made Lottie's glasses luminous as she smiled.

Thenie grimaced. "That is not what I—"

"He is aware of it, of course," her cousin said seeking out the man they discussed. "You'd have to be blind not to notice."

Notice? There was no doubting the man's allure. His square shoulders, and tall and commanding demeanor contrasted Boothe, who stiffened with resignation at the sign of trouble. And then there was Wright-Smythe's intriguing eyes, sources of life that siphoned her will.

"I have to agree. There is something about him I cannot quite explain," Lottie went on. "He was a student of my father's, thin and gaunt, quiet and pensive. I thought to never see him again after Grey disappeared. The field of antiquities is not for the faint of heart, especially during war." She paused, nodding her thanks to several fanning ladies who offered congratulations on her marriage as they strolled about the room. "But exploration," she said softly. "Ah, but it brought out the flair I thought him lacking. He has thrived on deprivation, isolation, and investigation so much so that I would hardly recognize him at all save for Grey's brilliant and clever memory."

She listened intently, longing to know more about the man who stirred her senses, forcing herself not to become too enamored. She didn't need an adventurer or another relic hunter in her life. She needed security, a promise of tomorrow for her sisters. Papa and her uncle's activities abroad had denied them time, making them suffer the unthinkable a hundred times over, never knowing whether the two men would return safely or if she would be forced to be the harbinger of bad news to her cousin.

"Do you not find him handsome?" Lottie asked, shocking her to her slippered feet.

Stand firm. "I prefer a man grounded in permanence."

"Change is the only constant in life, Thenie." Lottie quipped.

"What a horrid thing for you to say, Lottie, as you've been whisked here and there and cast aside throughout your life. You are the last person in the world I'd expect to encourage me to take an interest in a man like Wright-Smythe."

"But I understand the allure now," she said, "the passion and ecstasy, the adoration and expectancy gripping our fathers." She bit her lower lip, fighting for words. "Thenie, I have seen wonders that stir the core of my very soul. If you could only gaze up at the columns of Athena's temple—"

"I thought you understood. Now, I see that you are just as misguided as our fathers have been."

Lottie stopped to say, "I have lived a lifetime in the past six months."

A piercing pain gripped Thenie's heart. She revered Lottie and Grey, and their nearly decade's old passion, appreciating the love they shared, the heartbreak and triumph, and the risks they'd taken to live life on their own terms.

"We are more alike, you and I, than you believe." Lottie pulled her close. "I know it. My aunt knows it. Though I cannot, for the life of me, understand why you act as if you are unaware. Something has happened while I have been gone, something unnatural and worrisome. But never you fear. I am back, and I am going to find out what it is and restore you to your former self."

"Lottie, I—"

"Shhh. Everything will be well." She glanced around the room, studying the dancing couples. "Perhaps it is *I* who has changed. Six months is a long time and I have discovered myself with Septimus." She straightened the brim of her glasses. "I suppose marriage, and traveling the world, does that to a person."

"*You* are a sight for sore eyes." There was no way Thenie would allow Lottie to think she was to blame for her present attitude. "You have never been able to say or do anything to alter my impression of you, or Grey. The truth is I have taken a wrong step forward. I will tell you everything when the time is right."

"Promise me," Lottie pleaded.

"I promise."

"We shall put things to rights, you and I. And if we cannot, then Septimus can."

"I should like that . . . very much," she said. If there was anything to be done, her cousins could do it.

Lottie smiled past her. "Speak of the devil."

Grey begged Thenie's forgiveness and swept Lottie away to speak to a couple at the refreshment table. Boothe watched Thenie from his position there, shifting his stare when their gazes locked to a group of young ladies seeking his attention.

Had she made a horrible mistake in rejecting him?

"*I am determined, come what may, that my life will not be ruined by a kiss.*"

"*Who have you kissed, Miss Steere?*"

"*No one,*" she had said, though he had refused to listen. Instead, he had bolted out of the library, fuming, got entangled in a row with several gentlemen then let his accusations fly.

The gossip had multiplied before she'd even exited the library.

Augusta and Delphi had made it very clear, and in no uncertain terms, that it was her duty to marry so they could have their turn. Initially, they had encouraged her attachment to Boothe and expected an announcement of her betrothal to be made by Season's end. That would never happen now after the scandalous events at Mrs. Beaumont's ball. Besides, she did not love Boothe. Not in the way that Lottie and Grey demonstrated affection and attentiveness. She longed for earnestness, titillation, and fidelity.

Boothe's lack of civility proved he was incapable of loving her the way she yearned to be loved.

In Lottie's case, she had given up on marriage after losing the love of her life. And the transformation from determined woman and devoted daughter to happily married wife had been a joy for Thenie to witness. The natural shift in Fate had elevated Lottie's position in Society from professor's daughter to Lady Grey.

A viscount's daughter had fewer alternatives, however. The shallow *ton* demanded appearances be upheld at all times. She was the vessel of her parents' hopes—currency. They needed her to marry soon and well, so that the process could continue from generation to generation. And though Mama understood Thenie's hesitancy to marry, she supported Papa's directive, urging Thenie to choose wisely.

Boothe's yearly income exceeded £3,000 a year. His connections to politicians in high places made him a favorite at gatherings. His ambitions earned him high praise. With the war at an end, and more and more men returning from the continent, an alliance of their two families would have been celebrated.

That alone would have been enough for the old Thenie, who, by the by, would never have pondered kisses in public. But after observing true love, how could she settle for anything less?

CHAPTER FIVE

I, who was an eye-witness of the event, can testify to you, that though Miss S is rumored to have been kissed, she lost her ends in that design; the very life of female ambition; and those bright eyes, which are the bane of others shall always have the good fortune to live under Poseidon's protection. You will therefore forgive me, that I strive to conceal every wrong step made by any who have the honor to wear petticoats; and shall at all times do what is in my power, to make all mankind as much their slaves as myself. If my sex would consider things as they ought, that it is their fate to be obedient, and that the greatest rebels only serve with a worse grace.

—The Morning Post

M AKING HER WAY to the veranda, Thenie bristled with indignation as a hand divided her from the crush.

"A half-penny for your thoughts."

Were thoughts worth so little? "Only a half-penny?"

"It is just an expression," Wright-Smythe said. "Do not take offense."

"That seems inevitable, sir, when you are near."

A footman passed; his tray laden with more champagne. Wright-Smythe removed two glasses and offered one to Thenie. "Come. Come. Do not be so disagreeable. Allow me to make amends. This night is dedicated to your cousin, is it not? And the moon is too beautiful to waste."

He was right. It was a glorious night, which was why she'd worked her way to the veranda. The moon shone down on the gardens, brandishing an ethereal glow on flora and fauna. Making the night even more romantic, torchère's were stationed along the footpaths. Gow's Band played a piece by Handel magnificently, filling the house with happy contentment to accentuate the floral arrangements, abundance, and people and laughter. More comforting was the slight breeze emanating from the open veranda doors, chasing away the heat radiating off beeswax and the crush.

"I'd like to suggest a challenge to ease the boredom, if I may," he said.

"I don't recall admitting to being bored."

"You do not have to say it. The truth is in your eyes."

Was it true? Had she let down her guard? "If I am disinterested, what do you propose to boost my morale and march me back into compliance?"

"One word. Chance." His stare narrowed irresistibly, making her fight to hide her arousal. "A game," he continued when she failed to understand.

Warning bells clanged in her brain. Had she been too generous to trifle with him? "My home is not a gaming hell." Cradling her champagne glass, she chewed her bottom lip, unnerved but slightly tempted to hear more. Dallying with Wright-Smythe would be a distraction, yes, but a dangerous diversion Mama, her sisters, and even Lottie would warn her against. "What type of game?" she asked hesitantly.

"Two players." The words tumbled out of his mouth as if he'd proposed such a pastime before. She sipped her champagne. "Winner gets his or her heart's desire."

Her throat seized. She coughed. "Heart's . . . desire?"

What could that possibly mean? She searched the faces of the couples around them, praying no one had overheard his scandalous suggestion. And yet, in spite of the shock and the worry, the excitement and suspicion influenced her mind in ways she never thought possible. Was she really going to consider it, after—

"Yes." His searching eyes and nearness silenced everything but the sound of her beating heart as she waited for him to explain further. "The winner gets a kiss from the loser."

"*The winner gets a*—" She set her glass down on another footman's tray, fearing she'd imbibed too much champagne. Surely, she had not heard him correctly. And this after she'd contemplated what it was to be kissed and that very thing had caused her ruination . . . Oh, but Wright-Smythe was ruggedly handsome, a devil in disguise, was he not? He stood, glaring down at her with an air of superiority and intelligence she found difficult to resist.

Oof! It was getting harder to resist him.

A niggling idea scuttled through her brain. What would it be like to kiss a man like Wright-Smythe?

He is a relic hunter, a man willing to do and say anything to get what he wants. Her knees nearly buckled at the thought that this man wanted something from her.

But what?

Naturally, she'd have to refuse his offer. The game he suggested was shocking, inconceivable. The thrill of kissing him was far more potent than the idea of kissing Boothe had been, and the act called to her with abandon.

Heavens! Her spine tingled as his gaze held hers and he waited patiently for her to answer. What could she say? What was a proper young lady to do? Propriety demanded a refusal to such buffoonery. He grinned, reading her like a book. She stared at his lips, practically falling into a swoon as she wondered what kissing him would feel like—repugnant or rewarding, titillating or devastatingly inadequate.

A seed of indecision sprouted inside her, deliberate in its search for life-sustaining loam. Boothe lingered in the corner of the ballroom, chatting away with several politicians, ignorant of her plight. Mama and Papa were entertaining a duke and duchess. Lottie and Grey were dancing and laughing. Augusta and Delphi were sitting along the wall like wilted flowers dependent on rain.

"Very well. I'll play your game." Almost immediately, she realized she had no idea what the game was. She hiccupped. *Oh dear!* "What is it called?"

"It is an amusement as old as time itself."

His enthusiasm weakened her knees. She swallowed thickly, fearful of what she'd just agreed to do. "And how is this *amusement* performed?"

"I shall ask you a question and you must respond, truthfully. If you choose not to answer,"—his voice lowered an octave—"you must accept my challenge."

"You have tricked me, sir." She turned away as if to walk off without another word, but he grabbed her forearm and held her back. Stimulating sparks raced through her body, delivering a stronger punch than the champagne she'd imbibed. She turned her angry eyes on him. "What you suggest is not a gentleman's game."

"I assure you. I *am* a gentleman."

"According to whom?" she asked skeptically.

"Myself." His soft chuckle plummeted her spirits. "Why do I need a title or the king's edict to prove myself? I am not anyone's invention, especially the *tons*."

"You know this is the way of things, a custom that protects gullible females."

His eyes narrowed. "You do not appear susceptible to me."

"No," she agreed with half-hearted determination. "I am not." Her uncle had toiled for years at Hadrian's Villa, earning a professorship at Cambridge without a title. He and Thomas Young had deciphered the

Rosetta Stone, a brilliant discovery that they hoped would lead others to read Egyptian script on the tombs buried throughout the desert. She was stronger and smarter than she realized, and she'd been raised to recognize the difference. "You have my cousin's trust and friendship." Here, she had him. "I am quite certain you would not jeopardize that bond."

"I will not." He scrutinized the room. "I am merely seeking alternate ways to entertain myself. As you said so yourself, I am not accustomed to Town and I have learned other ways of spending my time."

The words he threw back at her sickened her stomach. "If I agree to your *diversion*, when and where do you propose we begin?"

"Now." The mischievous gleam in his eyes hinted she would grow to regret agreeing to play his game. "Here?" she asked incredulously.

"And why not?"

She backed away, her future and the hopes of her sisters balanced on the precipice. Was she making a disastrous mistake? She couldn't afford more, certainly not the one she'd already made. And yet, invisible threads piloted her to Wright-Smythe for reasons she could not fathom. His invitation thrilled her senses. It allowed her a reason to be close to him, to hear his restorative voice, to believe she could be something more than a blight upon her family.

"Very well," she said. "I accept." She snatched up another glass of champagne from a passing footman. "But I insist, you go first."

"Brilliant," he said, grinning. "Let's begin."

"What do I do?"

"Answer my query or,"—he paused for effect—"accept a dare." She nodded that she understood, her heart pounding. "Very well. Let's start with an easy question. When was the last time you lied?"

She reached for her throat. "I object to this game."

"You agreed to play." The corner of his mouth twitched. "You do not intend to back out when we've barely gotten started, do you? I thought you were true to your word. Or are you as addlepated as the other young females gracing these halls with visions of grandeur flitting about in their heads?"

How dare he suggest—"Sir, my sisters are in attendance."

"Them, I exclude. I am only interested in *you*." He bobbed his head, accepted his own portion of champagne, then peered at her over the rim of his glass with a look that implied he found this whole debacle extremely entertaining. "Ergo the reason for the game."

If she satisfied his curiosity, would he take that knowledge and shame her before all and sundry? "I will not dignify your question with an answer."

"A dare, it is, then." A naughty gleam glinted in his eyes, her refusal to satisfy his curiosity giving him permission to make her do something untoward. She closed her eyes and prayed for salvation. "I confess, I find it hard to believe you'd chose a dare so soon."

"Humiliation is a great motivator."

He chuckled. "You could have easily offered something benign like 'she has brown hair' when her hair has been arranged to parade her golden locks to advantage."

Unamused, she stared at him in surprise. "Forgive me if I did not understand how this game was played."

SHE UNDERSTOOD PERFECTLY.

Spencer didn't know whether to be more impressed by Thenie's boldness or her conversational dexterity. Wisdom pointed to the latter the minute an idea struck him. How far was she willing to go to avoid the truth? And why?

Her defiant stare aroused his eagerness to test this theory. "Dare me," she said nervously.

"Very well," he said. "Let's start with something easy, lest you say I took advantage." He glanced about the room, a sense of recklessness taking over. After all, he was beholden to the Steeres for a place to sleep. But, being dead to the world—an inviting thought—brought him back around to Thenie. She stood before him like Athena carrying a spear and shield. The pearls decorating her hair were an understated substitute for the sphinx flanked by two griffins that ornamented the original goddesses' head.

The tension between them heightened. "Pick a couple dancing," he said. "Say two honest things about them."

"You hold back, sir." She searched the crowd, a triumphant smile ornamenting her face. "There. My cousin and her husband. See how they laugh gaily? One, they are deeply in love. And two, they make a striking couple."

She does know how to play the game. "I made that one too easy for you."

"Did you? I fear I am still trying to comprehend the rules." Her steely jaw and defiance sharpened as the music crescendoed.

"Allow me to instruct you." He swallowed hard, eager to test Thenie's limits, and unsure how fast he should take this latest jest. "Let's continue. What is your biggest fear?"

She stiffened. "I fear nothing."

"May I remind you of the circumstances of our bet? Or does being kissed before all and sundry appeal to you?" He could see it didn't, that the very idea heightened her alarm. The permanency and purity of that knowledge germinated inside him on a biological level, instructing him to take care. "What will it be? Truth or dare?"

Thenie licked her dry lips then glanced away.

Ah. She toyed with the idea of kissing him. Perhaps that is why she accepted his diversion rather than continue her ruse of pretending to enjoy herself.

"Another dare, then," he said. Nothing humiliating, of course. He could soften the blow there at least. After all, he was not a cad, even if he'd been accused of being one. "Go to the refreshment table and drink another glass of champagne."

She shot him a look of disgust.

"Yes. I know. I am going easy on you, again. Humor me, will you? I am trying to prove to you that I am a noble fellow."

"Impossible. I cannot play the game if I am deep into my cups, sir." Her eyes narrowed, her mouth thinning. "Unless that is your goal. And to think I was just about to call you a gentleman."

"What changed your mind?" He cocked his brow, his curiosity mounting. "Have I not proved beyond a doubt that your safety is paramount?"

"The jury is out on that score." She made an effort to straighten the delicate lace edging on one of her gloves. "I am more determined than you might think to win this game of yours, however."

"Brilliant." That is what he was hoping for—a challenge.

Not to be beaten, Thenie straightened her shoulders, and set off for the refreshment table. Halfway there, she picked up a glass of spirits, turned, and deliberately drank the entire contents in front of him. "There," she said, her eyes glazing.

A mixture of guilt and pleasure warred within him. How far would Thenie go to win this game?

"Do your worst," she said as she strode back to him, weaving slightly with an audible slur in her tone.

"What is the naughtiest thing you've ever done?"

THENIE CONTEMPLATED WRIGHT-SMYTHE'S question. She'd done

several things she wasn't proud of in her lifetime, but only one in particular rushed to the forefront of her thoughts.

"My life will not be ruined by a kiss."

She'd done many things she regretted—blaming her father for entertaining possibilities. Criticizing her mother for not telling Papa to return from faraway lands. Detesting the dishonesty of others and refusing to admit that she was part of the problem.

"What is the wickedest thing I have ever done?" Resolve surged through her. She inhaled deeply to steady her legs and boost her confidence, praying this next challenge would not involve another glass of champagne. "I prefer the dare."

"You are not making this easy." His exasperation triggered something deep inside—a desire to have her passions quarried and treasured like the most precious of relics any hunter had ever found. "And your rebellion is disappointing."

"I am not rebelling against you, but the labels Society places upon my sex." Why should she share her inmost secrets with this man? It would be sheer lunacy to do so. He was just going to disappear, like Papa, like her uncle . . . like Lottie. *"When a man undertakes to do his own business, it is not likely that he will be disappointed."*

"Aesop. Impressive."

Funny how she quoted Aesop now, when in reality it was something her mother and Lottie were fond of doing. "It is an inherited attachment." Her heart hitched, a deep dark yearning to seek help anywhere it can be found haunting her with abandon. *"I'm not fool enough to give up certainty for an uncertainty."*

"But doesn't Aesop also say: *'Honesty is the best policy'*?" He lowered his voice. "Does it not trouble you where this game is headed?"

Unquestionably. Though there was a tiny part of her that wanted to lose, that desired to taste his lips. Ashamed of her thoughts, she lowered her half-lidded gaze.

"Admit it," he said. "You are incapable of telling the truth."

"Are you daring me to lie?"

"Why should I?" His voice deepened with a heaviness that set her teeth on edge. "Are you so reckless that you would do anything to resist me?"

"I am ready to defy anyone." Her legs weakened with the thought. "My pride will not allow me to concede, sir." Not when her reputation, and her sisters' reputations depended on the outcome.

"You do not understand, Thenie. The price of this game is more than a kiss." He tilted her chin with his thumb, sending a shot of heat through her body as he raised her face to meet his. "You'll learn soon enough that I am determined. Keep that in mind as you reevaluate the terms of our bet."

"The terms were set, and I agreed. I do not need time to reconsider—"

"Reconsider what?" Lottie swept in to take Wright-Smythe's place when he annoyingly vanished into the crush at her appearance.

"Viewing the Marbles," Thenie said, hoping to distract Lottie from what was really going on. A rare occurrence, if she succeeded, because her cousin had such a quick mind.

"The Marbles?" Lottie nodded to several ladies strolling about the room, each waving fans and trading remarks. "I am seeking out Wright-Smythe. Didn't I just see him with you?"

Here, she opted for truth. "I believe he saw someone of his acquaintance."

"Oh? I wonder who." Lottie strained to see over the crowd. "Did you see where he went?"

Thenie inclined her head to the refreshment table, having narrowed her gaze upon his large frame towering above the other men. "He is there."

How easy it had been to locate him.

"Lovely. Then I must away. As to the Marbles, I shall endeavor to convince Septimus to speak to Papa. Perhaps a showing could be arranged for you, if that is your wish." She turned to regard the lively room—the bobbing couples, delightful laughter, and the riveting parade of mingling guests. "I should like very much for you to view them. Though, they might be too suggestive and scandalous for your sensibilities."

She pursed her lips. "I *am* a woman grown."

"Indeed. But the delicacy of the matter is that the style defines heroes in idealistic poses." Lottie bent closer, concealing the discussion behind her fan. "Imagine them. Slumbering in darkness, stretched and compressed. Refined and persuasive, the statues labor and strain against the stone, longing to be free, revealing human desire and deceit in quiet intimacy. The spectacle is quite breathtaking."

"We have both reflected on the Lansdowne Herakles, and there were no repercussions."

"There are . . ." Lottie raised her fan higher, isolating the two of them from prying eyes, "nudes in repose, Thenie. Positions of ecstasy depicted in each frame."

Hardly able to visualize the erotic scene or gauge what her reaction might be to the sight, Thenie shivered breathlessly, praying no one noticed the color rising to her cheeks. It made perfect sense now—the attention given the Marbles. Classical beauty had inspired poets like Byron and talented artists ever since the dawn of time.

"I can see you are determined, and that pleases me. I'll have Septimus make the arrangements with Lord Elgin. But . . . before I go off in search of our friend, how are you and he getting on?"

Momentary panic seized Thenie. Would her cousin be horrified to learn that she'd agreed to play Wright-Smythe's tawdry game? *Oh, yes. I've been very naughty.* "We are continuing to get acquainted, though, I daresay, he is learning more about me than I of him. I've never met a more curious man."

"I shall speak to him."

"No," she said too quickly. "Please. Do not admonish him. In our every encounter, he *has* been a gentleman." And how it pained her to admit it. "Forgive my agitation. My mind is elsewhere tonight, that is all."

"You are right in one regard," Lottie admitted to Thenie's surprise. "Except—" Had she heard the rumors? Was this the moment her world came crashing down about her? "I find you . . . altered."

Lottie swept her close, interlocking their arms. Lord and Lady Borringdon gathered before the Earl and Countess of Manners. Nearby, the feather in Mrs. Beaumont's turban as she passed by in a flourish, fluttered about her face. She could be heard complimenting the unequalled grandeur of the room.

Mama had triumphed, yet again. But would this be the last time?

"Life has been a whirlwind since your arrival," she said. "All any of us needs is rest."

How was that possible given the heavy burden weighing on Thenie's shoulders and the fantasies commandeering her mind? Lord Elgin's Marbles were tangible objects, easily discarded. But Wright-Smythe was real—here, now—and this game of his had hardly begun.

"There will be time for rest later." Gow's band struck up another waltz. Lottie's face grew more animated as she spied her husband conversing with several fashionable men. "For now, pardon my retreat, Thenie, but Septimus promised me this dance. I do love the Marquis of Queensbury Medley. Oh, but I dare not leave you alone—"

"Off with you." She would have to be cruel, indeed, to deny her cousin a dance with her true love. "Go. Enjoy your husband. I should check on my sisters."

"Why, they are dancing this set." Stepping away, their hands barely clasping, Lottie continued, "You should have been there. I mentioned I was disheartened that there were empty dances on your sisters' cards and Septimus enlisted every eligible bachelor in the room to the cause—making sure no one added their name twice. You cannot imagine your sisters' horror and excitement."

Oh, but she could. And did. "Thank you." She offered her cousin a smile. "Go to your husband. You need not worry about me. There are several people I'd like to speak to nearby."

Liar!

"If you are certain." She wasn't, but Septimus waited for Lottie and rounds of applause increased the expectation for her cousin's appearance.

Augusta and Delphi looked up at their dance partners, beaming, their festooned hair bobbing as they waited for the music to begin. Thenie swayed slightly under the strain of Lottie's absence, pondering their fate. Was this to be her sisters' last ball? Was she going to be the reason they had to settle for marriages of convenience?

The champagne invigorated and brilliance beamed from the chandeliers, the chains supporting the crystals and dripping beeswax candles as precarious as her malleable plight.

Her sisters' future husbands would have to be above reproach, naturally. Suitable, honorable, insistent that they were pure and virtuous. Papa's reputation, alone, would ensure they were well provided for. *As for me?* She'd agree to marry any man as long as he did not place limitations on the inner workings of her mind, or her comings and goings. A strong order, to be sure, but a gift many wives received after providing an heir and a spare.

If I do my duty . . .

Her future husband would have to be a man with no intentions to travel abroad, one free of the all-consuming urge to study antiquities and ascertain why empires fell. He would have to be a man who honored the duties of his station, attending the House of Lords, clubs, parties and the like, allowing her every opportunity to care for her sisters and any future children they would ultimately sire.

Children.

Heat edged up her neck. *Merciful heavens!* How did one provide an heir and a spare? And . . . if the very thought of conceiving a child made her blush, how was she going to find the courage to observe the Marbles?

Or—*Saints preserve her!*—if she won this game, how was she supposed to kiss Wright-Smythe?

CHAPTER SIX

*See the uncertainty of human affairs! The beaux, the wits, the
gamesters, the coquettes, and the gallants, all now follow Miss S's
debate, pining for Fate's kiss. Such is the state of things when a man
in want of a wife needs one pure of heart and none can be found.*

—The Morning Post

S EVERAL DAYS PASSED before the townhouse was unreservedly put
back to rights. Mama's ball was a triumphant success, declared *The
Morning Chronicle*, comparing it memorably to Lady Caroline Barham's
ball in March. Hot house flowers were distributed to the sick, and
leftover food was delivered to the Dials. Thenie's sisters regaled the
family with stories around the breakfast table, detailing the waltzes
they'd danced and with whom, never knowing Grey skillfully
concealed his part in the matter.

Thenie, on the other hand, was greatly distracted. She had not
seen much of Wright-Smythe since the ball, owing to the fact that
she spent the majority of her daylight hours helping Mama with her
philanthropic work on the East End. There, numerous work houses
fought to support the many migrants still flocking to the city for hope
of a better life.

Although Hyde Park was open to the masses, it was there, with
gravel crunching underfoot, that Thenie understood the difference

between the classes most. Thither, she and Lottie discussed the weather, the beauty and breadth of Hyde Park, while contemplating the serenity of the Serpentine as they took the air.

"What a splendid morning." Idle conversation and the sun beaming above had successfully fended off her doldrums. Sleep, of late, had been as elusive as securing her reputation or understanding Wright-Smythe. Lack of it dulled her body and slowed her brain, making her feel dimwitted. "Hopefully the rest of the day will prove as invigorating."

"We shall make it so," Grey said.

Every now and again, carriages rolled past on Rotten Row, stopping occasionally for passengers to exchange greetings. The sky was brighter, bluer in the park in stark contrast to the sooty air clouding the skies over the city, the very reason people flocked to this grand common to escape to green meadows and natural landscapes.

Birds chirped happily, swans—royal birds—swam in the river, their graceful white necks bobbing, the scene relaxing and tranquil. Inwardly, Thenie smothered the guilt plaguing her spirit, praying unceasingly that her secret would never reach the gossips of Mayfair.

But they had.

The silence between the cousins swelled the farther they walked, flora and fauna owning their attention. The sight of unhurried water and pendulous foliage enhanced the intimacy.

"You would like Athens as much as I do, Thenie," Lottie finally said, stifling a yawn. "The Serpentine reminds me of the peaceful, happy mornings we spent there. Dawn cresting over the horizon. Merchants gathering in the marketplace. The sounds of everyday life teasing the far reaches of the mind. Temples illuminated by the sun cast an authoritative shadow on the comings and goings of communal life."

"A scene like many others in the Mediterranean," Grey added. "Especially in Rome, where wealth and security have given way to war time and time again. Nevertheless, the air is salty and pure in fertile basins, and the people hang onto life there, heartily and happily dancing in the midst of trials, poverty, and despair."

Thenie listened intently, envying her cousins their travels, inquiring more about Athens and the origin of the Marbles, particularly Wright-Smythe's activities in the area as they split from the trail and made their way down the riverbank. "I am more than curious."

"Yes?" Grey asked, acknowledging her overeager questions without missing a beat.

"About Athens." She bit her lower lip, considering how to ask about Grey's friend without drawing too much attention to herself. "How did you and Wright-Smythe run into each other there?"

Grey inhaled a deep breath. His expression tender, his thoughts turned seemingly introspective as his gaze locked with Lottie's, making her feel like there was something they were not telling her. "At the Temple of Athena."

"We were marveling at the immense size of the structure when our guide motioned to several men standing amongst the rubble near the entrance. One was speaking to the other. The second one, Wright-Smythe, whom I almost did not recognize, was emersed in sketching one of the pediments." Lottie took hold of Thenie's hand. "I cannot emphasize enough how delightful it was to meet someone Septimus knew, in Athens of all places."

"Wright-Smythe knows almost everything there is to fathom about the Marbles."

"And you saw them . . . in their natural habitat?" she asked, mimicking her uncle.

"The Marbles?" At Thenie's nod, he went on. "What hasn't been disfigured or stolen or carted off to places unknown. Antiquity dealers have nearly stripped the temple clean. Notorious dealers like Thomas Jenkins—a cleverer, more fortunate rogue I've yet to meet—sell fabricated or stolen goods to the highest bidders. The scoundrel has persistent patrons like Charles Townley, Gavin Hamilton, Reiffenstein, Kaufman, and Goethe who will stop at nothing to obtain the latest relic."

"And Wright-Smythe?" Thenie asked. "Where does he fit into all of this?"

"He's a good egg," Grey said. "One of the best. A man interested in nations and people. To put it mildly, he abhors the illegal exportation of ancient objects and left Cambridge to ensure Athens does not suffer like Egypt and Rome. He's made a fortune—"

"Look!" Lottie exclaimed, cutting him off suddenly. "Someone is approaching."

An unmarked black carriage moved slowly along the river before rolling to a stop before them.

"If you'll excuse me," Grey said, "I'll offer my salutations to the occupants and wish them a good day so we can be on our way."

"Do, Septimus," Lottie agreed. "But, I beg, do not be long. We promised my aunt we'd be home in time for the dinner party she's arranged for us."

Grey waved then turned away, hurrying to the coach, and leaving them to guess who lurked inside.

"Who do you suppose owns that carriage?" Thenie asked, unable to stave off her curiosity.

"I would not know where to begin," Lottie said toying with her reticule. "Anyone can hire an unmarked carriage."

"Yes, but . . ." Did she imagine the piercing stare studying her from across the distance? It was an odd feeling, really, to be the subject of an invisible set of eyes. That was the purpose of the promenade, of the theater, of ballrooms, and taking the waters in Bath, wasn't it?

To see and be seen.

Lottie peered at her husband and the coach. "Septimus must recognize the occupant for he is taking much longer than I'd hoped. Come." She withdrew some breadcrumbs from her bag then held out her hand and waited for Thenie to take it. "Let us feed the swans like we did when we were children."

"You remembered." Lottie's contagious spontaneity managed to alter Thenie's mood. "How long do swans live, do you suppose? Are they capable of recalling us?"

"Swans recognize their own," Lottie said. "However, I do not believe they live as long as we do. I have read mute swans can live thirty years."

"The average lifespan of a swan is seven years."

"Thenie!" her cousin exclaimed. "I am utterly surprised you know this."

"I do read." She giggled, feeling free and happy and wanting to bottle the moment so she could relive their promenade like drifting back in time while sniffing a familiar scent. "You are always a good influence on me."

"Well, we are only five and twenty. I should like to share many more years with you. And if mute swans were here when we were younger, there's a chance they might remember our younger selves. What say you?" She took off at a run, her bonnet ribbons flapping behind her. "Shall we find out?"

"Yes." Thenie laughed, her inhibitions gone as the wonder of being a child flashed across her memories and the joy of casting aside the worries of adulthood set in. "It is a public park. Think of the numerous passersby that venture to this exact spot. Surely, there are other kind-hearted souls who mucked up their boots in an effort to show these beautiful creatures they care."

Slowly convinced that the swans found nothing remarkable about them at all, they walked and skipped and traipsed along the riverside, resuming a natural rhythm, humming a lullaby Mama used to sing to them.

"Thenie."

"Hmmm?"

"Earlier, you asked us about Wright-Smythe. Have you formed an opinion of the man yet?"

She carefully skirted the question. "Why do you want to know?"

"We are like sisters, you and I. Nearly as close as Augusta and Delphi. And I know you better than you know yourself. I am not blind. I have seen the way you look at him, when you think no one is aware."

"He is conceited." The words flew out of her mouth before she could think better of replying at all.

"Proud and resilient, or rugged and persuasive." Lottie squeezed her arm, sinking into her with a familiarity that was both comforting and welcome. "Which describes him better?"

"I,"—what to reveal without giving too much away—"he . . . has a strange way of communicating."

"With you, or anyone else in particular? Personally, I have not found him strange at all. In fact, I find his passion for antiquities appealing, authentic . . . and *arousing*."

"Lottie!" Surely, her cousin teased for Thenie's amusement. She wouldn't dare describe Wright-Smythe in such a manner. He was a cad, a schemer. One didn't have to look far to see past his weathered veneer. "I agree only that he excels particularly when he speaks of the ancients." Sadly, she found no fault with him there. "But . . . if you must know. He has a habit of showing a lack of proper reserve in his dealings with me for my taste."

Lottie spun to face her. "Has he done something untoward?"

"No," she said, desiring to add. *Except for upending my resolve and increasing my anxiety. Blast the foolish game he convinced me to play, and the promise of a kiss that steals my breath and keeps me from sleeping at night.* She turned back to the river, unable to admit her shortcomings, ghastly as they were. "Oh, Lottie! He—"

"Isn't this a fine day and a picturesque place to greet friends and acquaintances?" *That voice!*

"I dare say it is," Grey confirmed with the same level of boyish enthusiasm.

Thenie crossed her arms and stared miserably at the swans, fighting to regulate the beating of her disloyal heart. She shouldn't have bothered. Her efforts to ignore Wright-Smythe failed. No matter what she did, the man simply couldn't be overlooked, if her body had any say.

His deep voice aggravated the uncertainty inside her. "It is a pleasure to see you again, Lady Grey and . . . Miss Steere."

Drat! Why had he joined them? And why was his chivalrous bow so alluring? All she had wanted was a peaceful walk outdoors with her cousins. Instead, she was forced to endure Wright-Smythe's presence. The wheels of the mysterious carriage engaged and horses' hooves struck the ground, clip clopping down Rotten Row, leaving her at his mercy.

"The pleasure is ours," Lottie said, springing toward Thenie and capturing her arm to intertwine it with hers. "And a fine day it is, indeed. Are we not lucky to have met you in the park like this?"

She shot a look at Wright-Smythe, nodding politely. He straightened his gloves as their gazes locked. "'Luck is the intersection of preparation and opportunity.'"

Grey snickered. "I believe that quote is Seneca's."

"'*Words may be deeds.*'" Lottie said, quoting Aesop. "But oh, what a brilliant reminder Seneca is of our time in Athens."

"Darling," Grey said. "On that note, you will be delighted to know that I have invited Wright-Smythe to dine with us this evening, and he has agreed on two conditions."

Thenie's heartbeat faltered, for it had been her hope to be rid of Wright-Smythe for good. "What conditions?" she asked, nearly breathless.

Grey arched a brow, cleared his throat, and dabbed at his pocket. "Let us move on and I'll explain."

Lottie winked at Thenie then took her place at Grey's side, interlacing her arm with her husband's. "Do go on."

"As to the first, he's agreed to attend as long as Cook can add another plate to Lady Steere's table tonight."

As Grey rambled on, a sense of abandonment struck Thenie keenly. Nevermind that she counted on her cousins to act as proper chaperones and protect her from men like Wright-Smythe. Summoning an iron will, she forced a smile on her face, nodding and agreeing to everything Grey and Lottie and their guest discussed, from the origins of the Serpentine, to its natural, snake-like design, and the firework display they'd missed the year before.

"And the second?" she asked with consternation.

"I will gladly sup with you, Miss Steere," Wright-Smythe said, "if you would find it in your heart to take a stroll with me this fine day." He moved closer to her, taking Lottie's place without reluctance. He placed his hand over his heart and bowed his head, the classic behavior of a gentleman that somehow seemed foreign and compulsory for a rugged looking man at the same time. "Allow me."

His polite probe impressed her even as she fought to ignore the damage his nearness did to her senses. It would be impolite to shame Grey's friend in her cousins' presence. Of course. Curtsying, she locked her arm in his, her heart pounding in her ears at the foolishness of her acquiescence and feeling completely disoriented by his nearness. "How can I refuse?"

He led her down the Row, past a cluster of trees, remarking on the excellent conditions of the oak, chestnut, and beech at their stations. Grey and Lottie lagged behind, providing Thenie and her escort ample space to converse without being overheard. Exactly the opposite of what Thenie required. And yet . . . a part of her yearned to learn more about this secretive, complex, tenacious man.

"I find myself most fortunate to be invited to sup with you all this evening," he called back over his shoulder for Grey and Lottie's benefit.

"Who am I to prevent you from breaking your fast?" Thenie asked before silently pleading for Lottie's help.

"Do continue walking ahead," Lottie said, ignoring her. "We shall not be too far behind."

"Shall we?" Wright-Smythe lifted a well-placed brow, his eyes gleaming intensely. Several quiet moments passed, each one suspended by the hitching of her breath and the increased rhythm of her heart. "Is it your usual habit to chase swans?"

"No." She gave herself leave to laugh, finding his bewilderment somewhat endearing as she pictured him running after swans in oversized boots. "We delighted in the act as children—to our detriment—excluding the skinned knees and soiled clothes that earned our governess's disapproval."

He smiled, a perfect dimple forming in his cheek charming a pathway to her heart. "You should laugh more, and often."

She glanced away, pretending to study the light reflecting off the motionless river, the sum of her warming to this gentle side of him. "I do enjoy a good laugh."

It was the first honest thing she'd said since they'd met. And the intimacy of confiding in him felt decent and right.

"Laughter should be required by every man, woman, and child. Every. Single. Day."

"Thus, making the world a more enjoyable place to live?" she asked, knowing the answer.

"You make light of it, but laughter," he said, "is the one emotion to be cherished above all others, except love, of course. You cannot find a more priceless, stimulating, and curative sentiment."

Love. How easily Wright-Smythe spoke of the emotion. Her mouth went dry, her mind whirling. "And have you,"—she lowered her gaze to his mouth, trying to remain deceptively calm—"ever been in love?"

A chill surrounded them, the sounds of their footfalls filling the air.

"I never desired the feeling until I heard laughter depart from your lips."

She stopped in her tracks, nearly tripping over her skirts, a pulsing knot of anxiety swelling to life inside her. "Sir!"

"Shhh." He glanced back at Lottie and Grey, intonating that everything was all right before taking her arm and leading her once more alongside the riverbank. "We have not finished our game yet."

"No," she said, studying his full mouth, and glorying in the strength of his forearm as his muscles hardened beneath his sleeve. He had not forgotten their bet. Neither had she. A sane woman never forgot the promise of a kiss. "We have not."

"I must confess." He turned his smile up a notch. "I am looking forward to claiming my prize."

Her thoughts ventured back to the moment he'd suggested their game, making her astonished by the power he had over her. "But what if *I* win?"

CHAPTER SEVEN

*As for the dear daughters like Miss S committed to our care, let
sobriety of carriage, and severity of behavior, be such, as may make
that noble Lord B, who is taken with beauty, turn his designs to such
as are honorable. Make us joyful mothers of a numerous and wealthy
offspring, and let our daughters' carriages be such, as may bless
happy marriages, from the singularity of life, in this loose and
censorious age in the exact manner of Aphrodite: a sincere convert to
everything that's commendable in fine young ladies.*

—The Morning Post

HOURS LATER, SUPPER was a casual affair in the Steere household,
except when formal parties were held on the premises.

"I heard the oddest story today at the Haberdashery where I am
having a new hat made."

Aghast, Thenie stared at Augusta, wringing her hands in her lap.
She had accompanied her sisters to the first floor, happy to discover
their parents were already in attendance. She closed her eyes, feeling
worthless and wicked and fearful of what Augusta was about to say.
What had she heard? Her heartbeat made a mad dash. Her throat
ached and a stab of guilt brought her acute physical pain.

Papa grumbled. "You know I do not recognize tittle-tattle, Augusta. Especially at the dinner table."

Delphi giggled. "I'm sorry, Papa. I cannot help myself. It isn't every day we hear you use the word, *tittle-tattle.*"

Papa frowned, his frustration mounting.

Augusta and Delphi were famous for eavesdropping, but Delphi was the most prolific gossip in the family. Ever eager to discover news about the *ton*, she set out to prove her betters were just as normal as the merchant and working-class sector. "As for what we heard at the haberdashery,"—she angled a glare at Thenie—"Well. It saddens me to say that Augusta may not need a new hat this Season, after all. As Lottie and Mama like to say, *'you could always have more, but you could also have less.'* And in this instance . . ."

"No more." Papa leaned forward, his hand poised mid-air as he reached for the wine glass one of the footmen had just filled for him.

"You heard your father." Mama raised her hand to quiet the twins, who began and finished each other's sentences so fast no one could make sense of their complaints. When that didn't work, she asked, "What does this tittle-tattle have to do with our family?"

"Everything." Augusta's stare pinned Thenie to the back of her chair. "One of us, in particular."

Thenie tried to hide her mortification as Augusta's accusation hovered inappropriately around, above, and below them. Whatever her sister had heard, she prayed that Augusta would get it over with before Wright-Smythe and her cousins arrived.

"Thenie?" Mama asked sternly. "Do you have something to tell us?"

"Nothing of significance." She reached for her wine and sipped at it with all the patience she could muster. Then, clenching her jaw, she swallowed back the sob that formed in her throat, aware that her family observed her discomfort in speculative silence. The moment she had dreaded with all her heart had come. "What have you heard?"

"Parthenia." The warning in her father's voice wasn't missed. "What have you done?"

"There are rumors making the rounds that a petite, blonde was seen in Mr. Beaumont's library reading Shakespeare."

"That is hardly a crime," Mother said. "I have done that very thing when boredom sets in."

"Except this specific young lady admitted brazenly, 'I cannot save myself.' She said that 'the *ton* would find out about *the kiss* and I will be scandalized.'" *I did say that, heaven help me.* "And there's more."

"More?" she asked dumbfounded. She prayed that they didn't know about the game she played with Wright-Smythe. That would be the nail in the coffin.

"Oh yes," Augusta's voice lowered to a broken whisper. "Further, a blonde woman disgraced herself at Lady Cholmondeley's ball."

"She was seen raising her skirts in the countesses' maze," Delphi finished breathlessly, her hand dramatically held over her heart.

Thenie blinked. Surely, her sisters did not think she was capable of doing such a thing.

"Your sister has never been to Lady Cholmondeley's ball," Mama said in her defense.

"Others speculate that you are none other than the blonde who was caught in the rakish arms of a marquess in the Duke of Rox-burgh's stables."

Thenie stood so quickly, her chair scrapped the hardwood floor. She couldn't just sit idly by while her sisters teased her cruelly. "Papa . . . Mama. I am sorry, but Augusta and Delphi are spreading the type of tittle-tattle servants pass along from one residence to the next." She inhaled deeply, determined to make things right. She was tired of hiding the truth for fear of what it would do to her sisters. "I do have an admission, however." Her stare was bold as they gazed at her expectantly. "My relationship with Lord Boothe is at an end."

"Thenie!" her sisters shouted.

"What have you done?" Papa asked.

Augusta railed. "This is a travesty!"

"But . . ." Delphi labored to breathe. "You know how much we depend on you to marry first. I am the last to wed. How long must I wait?"

"I did—" The twins had the presence of mind to look away so she could continue. "I thought," she went on to explain. "Once, I wanted to marry Boothe. He is a dashing fellow, a good dancer, eloquent and forthright. At least I thought he was until—."

"Until what?" Papa asked frowning.

"Truth be told, I simply do not love him. You see, after Lottie and Grey reunited and I saw how happy they were, I realized admiration was not enough to sustain a marriage." Flatware disturbed a plate. The door to the dining room grated against the hinge, making her fear her cousins and Wright-Smythe had arrived to the sound of her dialogue. "I want what you have, Mama. What Lottie and Grey have. If I have to settle for less, I will not marry at all."

Papa pounded his fist on the table. "I have three daughters to wed. Not one. You are twenty-five. We do not have the luxury of time for you to continue putting off your responsibility. Your sisters cannot marry until *you do*."

Augusta and Delphi had the decency to look away. She pressed her lips together in abject misery. Knowing that her actions had disappointed her parents and stolen her sisters' hopes and dreams cut her in two. It was a hopeless situation made more malevolent by the animosity flowing between her and Boothe. There was no point in admitting that she was, indeed, the woman in Mr. Beaumont's library. Worse, she'd made a bet with Wright-Smythe, the victor winning a kiss. But how could she admit this without jeopardizing her reputation?

God help her, the damage had been done. The dilemma was in finding a way to keep it from affecting her sisters. Would they hate her forever? Could she blame them?

Augusta and Delphi caused a stir as they stood in unison, as if prepared to bolt from the room.

"Nothing is at is seems," she said, desperation and impetuosity weighing heavy on her chest. "I assure you all will be well."

"Will it?" Papa asked, a spasmodic trembling taking hold. "You have no idea the lengths to which your mother and I have gone to protect this family."

Mama calmly said, "And look how brilliantly it has all worked out, husband."

"Until this moment." He smiled warily at Mama, the love between them evidence that what Thenie searched for was worth the sacrifice.

Only a love match would do for her. Besides, there were other ways to ensure her sisters did not reach four and twenty minus wedded bliss. They could enlist the help of the Black Widow of Whitehall, if the situation called for it. She had heard good things about the woman. She was diligent and discreet. If her father worried about the likelihood they would turn into spinsters, the appropriate thing to do was . . .

She grabbed her throat, aghast at her own inability to see through the veil of her pride. Any match made by Mrs. Bessie Dove-Lyon would not involve love. The matchmaker fit couples together like game pieces, a gamble she was unwilling to take. As a consequence, she was dooming her sisters to the very same fate she sought to prevent for herself.

Papa tore his gaze away from their mother and smiled at Thenie. "More thought should be given to finishing this exchange. I will need to know exactly what you have done so I can attempt to fix it. But," he gazed about the room to the footmen positioned in each corner, "This is a private matter, and it requires—"

"Lord and Lady Septimus Grey, and Mr. Spencer Wright-Smythe," Greaves announced as the door widened to allow their guests entry into the dining room.

"Sit down, girls," Papa ordered. "We shall finish our discussion later."

Augusta and Delphi glanced at each other. Augusta shot Thenie a look of disgust that penetrated deep into her bones. Mama clicked her tongue, a childhood clue for them to smile and don the charm.

Her sisters immediately obeyed, sitting back properly in their seats like obedient offspring. Except they were far more elegant and talented in the female arts than Thenie could ever hope to be, especially now that she'd lowered herself enormously in their eyes.

In the midst of the trauma, Papa forced a smile on his grim face when Lottie entered the room. Practically one of the family, her cousin instinctively knew something was wrong, however. She glanced at Thenie, a worrisome expression transforming her face. Thenie looked to the footmen who'd been present during their heated discussion. Soon, Cook and her staff would learn the particulars, with the entire household to follow.

When will my mortification end?

"Thank you, once again, for opening your home to us, Uncle," Lottie said as Grey escorted her to her seat. When she sat down, she smiled sweetly at Augusta and Delphi. The smile they returned was hard won, emerging unnaturally stiff and confirming there was, indeed, a problem. "Forgive us if we have interrupted something important."

Good heavens! She could not allow this discussion to continue in front of Wright-Smythe. Her sisters were heated enough. They did not need another to stir the pot.

"We were discussing the weather," she quickly said.

Augusta crossed her arms then rolled her eyes, Delphi conforming to the same.

Grey, an observant fellow, and a man to offer his opinion willingly, must have suspected something nefarious was afoot because he sought to soothe the emotions boiling under the surface. "The rain held off long enough for us to have a handsome walk in Hyde Park today."

"Yes." Lottie beamed. "We saw the swans, Aunt. Oh, you do remember them, don't you?"

"I do." Mama smiled warmly down at her niece. "So many happy years. I think about them often, wishing only that your mother could have been there to enjoy them too."

Grey, with his perceptive habits of stealth and forethought, led Wright-Smythe to his seat. Then, and only then, did the two men bow politely to everyone present before taking their places. Grey and Lottie next to her sisters, and Wright-Smythe exasperatingly close to Thenie. In fact, right beside her.

The scoundrel's size was boldly intimidating, his golden-brown hair gleaming in the candlelight as he filled the space beside her. His lips were firm and sensual against his bronzed skin, his smile strikingly white, his profile sharp and confident. The look in his eyes left little doubt that he suspected something scandalous had occurred in his absence.

Was he thinking about their game? Butterflies flickered to life inside her. A winning kiss? *Don't lick your lips.* Melting her inhibitions and stealing her breath?

Don't look at him.

Too late. A sigh escaped her, drawing his attention.

Blast his hypnotic blue eyes! They stoked an indefatigable heat kindling in the far reaches of her womanhood. She'd never felt the like before and was certain the sensation would betray her, providing her sisters more reasons to accuse her of outrageous conduct.

Oh, how she wished he would just go away.

But how long had it been since he'd first arrived and her life had been turned inside out? A week, more? His existence toppled her plans in the most phantasmic way, making her regret the moment she'd taken her life into her own hands at Mrs. Beaumont's ball. Though the Beaumonts were unranked, the wealthy merchants were the envy of Town. Their parties showcased hot house flowers, the best instrumentalist's money could buy, and a feast for nearly four hundred guests.

"I see we have interrupted something important," Lottie said sweetly, as wine was poured, the swishing sound of spirits swirling around each glass exotic and inviting in the quiet room.

"No." Mama was the first to deny wrongdoing. "I assure you all is quite well. Isn't it, my darlings?"

Augusta lifted her glass, hiding a frown. Delphi impetuously crossed her arms over her chest like an unruly child and tsked, avoiding Lottie's gaze.

How were they going to get through this meal without tearing out each other's throats? The answer was simple.

Thenie would have to beg her leave.

"I'm feeling light-headed." She attempted to rise from her chair. "Perhaps I should join you another time."

Wright-Smythe bolted out of his seat to join her, his eagerness to come to her aid tugging at her heart. "Allow me," he said taking her hand.

"Sit down," she insisted under her breath. "This meal is in your honor, and I shall only be gone a moment."

Another lie. She intended to run away, to claim a megrim and run as far as she could from the look of disappointment on her parents' faces. Surrounded by their barely-sheathed temperaments, she wanted—needed above all things—a comforting presence by her side, not the dour disappointment they obviously felt. But how could she, in all her selfishness, deny Wright-Smythe this opportunity to sup with his friends?

He provided the answer. "I go where you go."

"Please," Papa said, as if recognizing the dilemma, "do sit down. Cook has prepared a wonderful meal, and I am quite certain she will consider it an outrage if we abandon the table just as she is about to serve. You know she abhors a tardy table."

Wright-Smythe chivalrously held her chair as she lowered into it, his touch lingering on her arm a moment longer than necessary. She steadied her heart, worrying she'd earned her sisters' disdain. Could she blame them? All they wanted was households of their own to run.

Footmen scurried round the table, the first course—artichoke soup—served competently. Mackerel with fennel and mint arrived, the conversation ranging from rumors of war to Napoleon escaping from Elba in March to Prussians advancing along the Rhine. New deals were in place to enhance the British Museum, its exhibits, and the dealers who imported goods from the continent before a lull in conversation took hold.

Wright-Smythe leaned closer. "What has happened? It feels like I have walked into the gates of Pompeii after Mount Vesuvius' eruption."

"You know how families can be," she explained, preferring not to go into the details. "One moment gathered with the best of intentions, the next nipping at each other's heels."

"This seems more serious, ergo the Vesuvius analogy."

"'Tis nothing but a misunderstanding." He searched her eyes once more. A world of promise and hope and passion swirled inside his seasoned irises. She yearned to delve into his mind, to uncover *his* secrets, gain the knowledge of humanity he'd acquired, to share his archaeological encounters, experience the joy of discovering something new and unseen by human eyes for hundreds of years. "Truly."

Liar! What did it matter, a lie or the truth? He was going to return to Athens, and she'd never see him again.

The prospect of sleeping under the stars as Papa had done, sharing a bed beneath a celestial sky with the man she loved made her ache with envy and desire. Could one kiss remedy her plight, end this delusion that she could actually thrive on foreign soil? A dare had gotten her into this whole new world of ifs and what nots. Jumping into the fire burned, branding her with passion and uncertainty. Her behavior had sealed her fate and that of her sisters. Oh, the irony was not lost on her.

"Everything will be right as rain tomorrow."

His fingers wrapped around hers beneath the table, the warmth of his skin providing her the courage she lacked. "If you require help, just ask."

"Be careful what you wish for," she said softly, avoiding her sisters' cross looks.

Supper was served. Each course offered a diversion. Wright-Smythe cut a section of roasted meat for her. Sweet and savory pies filled with game and various fish covered the table. Vegetables dipped in a buttery sauce added to the feast with details of her cousins' expeditions contributing a welcome respite.

Finally, the most elaborate and expensive portion of the meal arrived—dessert, biscuits and macaroons with dipping wines and liqueurs, pistachio and barberry ices, and fruits and marzipan to help with digestion.

"Grey tells me, Wright-Smythe," Papa said, "that you are eager to see the Marbles."

"Yes, my lord. I was hoping to obtain Lord Elgin's permission before I arrive at the museum."

Thenie's father waved his hand. "That should not be hard to gain. Elgin has offered admittance to artists who spend entire days rendering drawings of the Marbles. I know him well and can put in a good word for you—as I have for my brother and Grey."

"Where is the professor?" Grey asked. "I expected him to join us this evening."

"Duty calls, I'm afraid. As you are aware, I am sure, teaching, field work, and the exhibits at the museum keep my wayward brother out of trouble." With that said, Papa laughed like a man hiding an indulgent secret.

Lottie did not join him.

Thenie came to her uncle's defense. "My uncle is dedicated to his work. If that be a failing, the whole of the kingdom would suffer."

Mama, ever the gracious hostess, agreed. "My brother-in-law is loyal to his employers at Cambridge and strives to earn his keep. He has forfeited a great deal in his lifetime, as has any man thirsting for knowledge of the ancients. I can think of no greater calling, except taking orders."

Grey brushed Lottie's hand, the sweet moment rendering Thenie speechless as she observed them and wondered about the source of the double meaning they shared. "My father *has* sacrificed so much."

"More than enough." Grey's quick response was true to character.

The brief moment stirred memories of Lottie's childhood that tugged at Thenie's heartstrings. Her cousin crying herself to sleep while Uncle toiled in dust and mud across the sea. Crawling into Lottie's bed numerous times a week to console her weeping cousin in her father's absence.

Growing up without a mother had been monstrously difficult for Lottie, though they had all done their best to serve as meaningful substitutes.

What would Lottie's mother say if she could see how beautiful and accomplished her daughter was now?

CHAPTER EIGHT

It is matter of much speculation among the beaux and oglers, what it is that can have made so sudden a change in Lord B, as has been of late observed on doting mothers who have so good a sense of the frailty of woman, and falsehood of man, that they resolve to keep their daughters in safety, against themselves, and all their admirers. At the same time, a gay inclination, curbed too rashly, would but run to the greater excesses for restraint. Know then, that the Misses S, with all their flirting and ogling, have strong curiosities, and are the greatest eavesdroppers breathing.

—The Morning Post

WEEKS LATER, FLORA and fauna decorated the entrance to Vauxhall Gardens by way of Westminster Bridge. At a cost of 3 shillings, 6 pence, the visual marvel was an immediate bewitchment for the senses, affording passersby with a hint of the lilting strains of Maria Theresa Bland's sweet voice drifting over the Dark Walk, the Orchestra and Organ buildings, pillared saloons and rotundas and Turkish tents, as a marvelous invitation to the masses.

Vauxhall had been an indulgence for over twenty seasons. A respectable park, once frequented by families, it now housed people of every persuasion and occupation under groves of trees. Fruit bushes and perfumed flowers lined each path. A spectacular balloon ascent drew many onlookers seeking a breath of fresh air in a city known for soot and scarcity. War and toil, however, had disemboweled Spencer of farfetched partialities. Aside from processions dedicated to Athena at the Acropolis in Athens, he found the sight of groves and crosswalks and cascades mesmerizing. The sounds ethereal, as much lullaby as symphonic, soothing and sweet.

He was unaccustomed to High Society's whims and felt like a fish out of water in a crowd of onlookers who devoured one another in judgment and awe. To be seen and heard all the rage as partygoers ate outdoors, drinkers carousing—perchance looking for trouble—and the spectacular show of over fourteen thousand lights mystifying invention and introduction.

These were not the scenes a wanderer like Spencer anticipated. A man like him, lowly and simple, was unaccustomed to flawless finery and desired no more than good company, beeswax and parchment, and interesting conversation to tolerate his days.

That wasn't entirely true. No one captivated him more than Miss Parthenia Steere. Her beauty, her love of family, and loyalty to her sisters proved she was a good match. She enjoyed dancing and laughing, discussing intellectual matters, all of which would provide any man with years of personal enjoyment. There was something in her eyes, too, that invited him in, whether by instinct or against her will, the outcome remained the same.

She was intrigued by him, and he, her.

But she didn't trust him. She resisted his charms when he merely wanted to get to know her better. Her rejection denied him the depth of character he sought to understand. Normally, he'd count his blessings, thanking the Fates that he wasn't attached to such a woman. Strangely though, when it came to Thenie, he was resistant to move on. It was as if a delicate thread of sinew connected their bones. It was a strong, inseverable force and haunted him keenly, in spite of the warnings that she was the talk of Town.

According to Grey, prior to his arrival, Boothe had been the only suitor that could possibly deter his efforts to win Thenie's heart. So, what had happened between them? Where had the rumors about Thenie kissing a man originated from? Was Boothe the reason Thenie's reputation lay in taters?

Jealousy gripped him, and he immediately took a dislike to the baron. Had she kissed him?

"What do you think about Vauxhall?" Thenie asked from her position beside him.

He glanced down at her upturned face, longing to explore her mind, her body, as they left the carriage and approached the magnificent entrance. Vauxhall had ruined many lives. More was rumored to have happened at Vauxhall between the opposite sex than anywhere else in Town. And yet, fashionable Londoners sought its meeting places and drawing rooms at least once every season.

"I think it's the perfect place to continue our game."

Her startling smile sank into him, deeper and deeper, rooting like a seed buried and sprouting to life. "I should like that, very much."

Surprised by the sudden change in her, he said, "Even if Vauxhall has a reputation as a pleasure garden?"

"Yes." Her calm acceptance caused him alarm. "However, I shall only take part if I may be allowed the same opportunities you are given."

What opportunity? "Equality is important to me."

He longed to tell her that he wasn't like other men. He had no use for dowdy women who cowered before men or played coy to get what they wanted. Such was the life for ladies prodded by matchmaking mamas in the marriage mart.

He'd seen it happen enough and it disgusted him.

A woman's body needn't be shielded under yards of silk. Neither should she be prevented from gaining access to libraries and editions of ancient wisdom to enliven her spirits. He wanted a woman who wasn't afraid to don a pair of trousers, to get her hands dirty, to follow him without question and bask in the contributions of their success. A woman who felt as much at home in the desert as she was sporting silk slippers in ballrooms and hobnobbing with politicians.

He wanted Thenie to know who he was and what he stood for. To encourage her to love him. But how did he do that without scaring her away?

"You will allow me to ask the questions?"

"I see no reason why you shouldn't be allowed your turn," he said.

"Capital." She cast a glance over her shoulder. He followed her gaze, seeing Grey and his wife conversing with a couple he had yet to meet. "Where to start." She raised a gloved finger to her lips, plumping the tissue gently along them, increasing his curiosity as to their softness. "Did you really meet my cousin and her husband by chance in Athens?"

The answer came easily, though he would not disclose that the Greys had an ulterior motive. "Yes."

"How?" she asked shyly. Should he remind her that Lottie had already explained how they met? "Tell me again."

He owed her his side of the story. "I was with my assistant at the time." Demmed if he didn't miss Baros. "We were surveying the temple, drawing illustrations to understand where the Marble's missing pieces belonged when your cousins arrived."

"And?"

"And," he repeated, happy to relive the encounter, "naturally I was focused on my sketches. My assistant Baros brought your cousins to my attention. I have to confess that, at first, I could not believe my eyes. It had been years since Grey and I had last spoken and he happened to have a beautiful woman on his arm. Not something I expected."

Music crescendoed in the fresh air as they continued on the Grand Walk, passing ladies wearing the latest fashions. Sycamore and Elm bordered the path. Hanging baskets full of decorative flowers hung from balustrades and columns, the atmosphere lush and inviting. "Because you did not expect to see him in Athens?"

"What?" Distracted by laughing guests in a supper room left of a rotunda, Spencer measured her sweet musing look. "No. Grey was often in the field until his father's death. You misunderstand. I did not expect to see him with a woman because the last time I saw Grey, he'd sworn never to marry."

"Never?" Her mouth formed an unpleasant twist. "May I ask why?"

Ahead, a twelve-by-fifteen-foot painting of Britain's seven year's war, was stationed for effect. He led Thenie past the spectacular canvas.

"Are we still playing our game?" he asked, suggestively. At her nod, he continued. "Grey insisted that if he could not marry your cousin, he would go to his grave without her. Ah, but isn't that a true expression of love?" He smiled in remembrance, recalling the magnificent sight of Grey and Lottie dwarfed by the temple's magnificent size. "It had never occurred to me that I would see the two of them together again. So, you can imagine my surprise when I looked up from my sketches and spotted them there. I particularly remember hearing Grey say, 'Walcot would be invigorated by this ruin, wouldn't he, Lottie?' Baros spoke with them, while I recalled—thunderstruck, mind you—that I once had a professor named Walcot at Cambridge who happened to have a daughter named Lottie."

"What an odd twist of Fate," she said. "To meet my cousins in Athens, of all places."

Did she suspect it too coincidental? She should know by now that if he didn't want to tell the truth, he would have taken a dare. He captured her eyes with his. "The archeological world is quite small. Even I am amazed by the people who cross my path daily in Athens. It was a bit of luck, coming across Grey as I did, and learning that he and *Little Lottie* had been reunited."

Her smile was radiant. "They are good people."

"The finest," he agreed.

Entertainers dressed like jesters opined then moved on to the sea of sightseers. A glance over his shoulder proved that Grey and his wife had put more distance between them. Then, almost in an instant—as if he'd imagined it—they disappeared behind a grove of trees near a set of Turkish tents. And for a moment, a black clad figure emerged then vanished behind a gazebo covered in ivy.

Were the Greys meeting the famed Black Widow of Whitehall at Vauxhall? He'd been under the impression Mrs. Bessie Dove-Lyon rarely made an appearance out of the Lyon's Den, least of all outdoors. The Greys did have connections, however. Jointly, they dealt with Thomas Jenkins and antiquities dealers. And Lottie's father and Thomas Young were steadfast protectors of the relics making their way to the British Museum. As such, Grey was in a position to learn as much as he could about the museum, its imports, and trade routes, namely Elgin's Marbles.

That brought him back to his original dilemma. How had Elgin managed to carry off and ship the Marbles to the British Isles without an Ottoman firman? And if he had procured one, why couldn't the Ottoman or the British Museum locate it?

And what immediacy drove them to speak to the widow? He'd heard the Black Widow of Whitehall had connections to nefarious people, as well as aristocrats and monarchs. An avid collector, Mrs. Dove-Lyon was no stranger to the antiquity market, the names of dealers and financiers tumbling off her veiled lips without study. The information she'd already provided him, paired with the Greys', was crucial to helping him understand Lord Elgin's role in dismantling the Temple of Athena and cutting Athens out of the profit.

Thenie's clear blue stare was direct as his head dropped out of the clouds. "You are not playing fair."

"Am I not?" She could not know his purpose for coming to London, unless her cousin had confided in her. Little Lottie wasn't one to expose secrets, especially her own.

"No." She nearly stumbled on a rock and with his help, quickly righted herself. "The rules are: I ask the questions and you—refusing to answer—must request a dare."

"A dare?" He stopped in his tracks and turned to face her. "I am not the one with something to hide." But he did have secrets—one, in particular, being the Grey's request to save Thenie's honor—though now wasn't time to divulge them. He winked at her broadly. "Why would I choose a dare over speaking the truth?"

"You are a man," she said as if his sex was a pox against him.

Bollocks! He perused her, head to foot, knowing he'd have to set her straight. "Has your father or uncle or cousins ever played you false in the past?"

"No." Her eyes widened and the stark disapproval on her face rendered him speechless. "Not that I am aware, but—"

"Has Boothe?"

Rawness flickered in her eyes before her composure and dignity were restored. She turned away, scrambling for words. "Boothe . . . is a good man."

"Who is not playing fair now?" he asked. "It was my understanding, your cousin expected you to be betrothed to Boothe when she returned from her Tour."

Several couples moved past them and the way grew congested, testing his patience. When the Walk cleared and they were alone once more, her expression turned unnerving—her face taut, her tight-lipped smile bleak and sour.

"A false impression that I did not encourage." She reached out to touch a blooming rose hedge then snatched her hand back, wincing. "Oh! Where are my cousins?"

"Let me see." He seized her hand, her yelp of pain sending shivers down his spine. "How badly are you hurt?"

"It is nothing," she said, her eyes glinting beneath the lamps as a droplet of blood began seeping through her fine, white kid glove. "I am well. Really, I am."

"I'll be the judge of that," he said. "The thorn may still be impaled in your finger."

Without another thought, he began removing her glove—one finger at a time. She sucked in a breath, casting worried glances over her shoulder. Her breath was warm and moist against his face as she pleaded, "This is most improper, Mr. Wright-Smythe."

"Is it?" he asked, lifting her finger to examine a pearl of blood beading at the tip, her discomfort twisting in his gut like spoiled meat. "I see no other way to assist you."

The thorn was, indeed, still lodged in her tender flesh. He plucked out the offending barb then looked over the length of her hand, and—desiring to take her mind off the pain—raised her finger to his mouth and suckled it.

Her barely masked pleasure disappeared in an instant but not before he felt her digit pulse in his mouth.

"How dare you." Her cheeks colored as she spoke, but her imploring eyes cried out for more. "Please. People are watching."

His blood pounded, the pleasure pure and explosive. He didn't want to stop there. He wanted to taste every inch of Thenie, just as Athena required to be praised and adored. Nevertheless, he understood the danger as she shuddered with humiliation.

"There," he said restoring her glove to her hand. "Your finger should be fine but I fear your glove is ruined."

"You are—" Her mouth dropped open. "How dare you take such liberties."

"It is all part of the game, Miss Steere. We are to each other what a thorn is to a rose."

Had she enjoyed the familiarity as much as he had? Why was she so ashamed to admit it aloud? "I do not understand."

Neither did he. When Lottie had suggested he marry Thenie, she had been a complete stranger to him. Except, from the moment they'd met, the sensation that he'd always known her had stuck with him, teased him, reeling him in with an unusual rush of excitement.

"How far are you willing to go to win this bet?"

Her aloof smile disarmed him as she cradled her finger. "Until I win."

"Until *I* win." Her amusement swiftly died as he went on. "I have answered your questions truthfully. Can you honestly say the same?" His words were kind, measured, tactical enough to warrant her acceptance of defeat. "Admit it. I won."

"The game is not over because you . . . because I injured my finger." She searched his face, the string of lamps hanging above them glinting in her eyes. "What are you really about? What do you want?"

"My prize." He spread his hands and shrugged. "A simple kiss."

"One thing is perfectly clear." She watched him warily. "Nothing in life is simple."

Gossip had disrupted Thenie's life but marrying him offered the perfect solution to both their problems. He desired a wife. She needed a husband, a protector, someone capable of silencing the rumor mill. "Life, with all its complications, has powerful benefits."

"You c-cannot possibly expect me t-to kiss you here," she said casting fretful glances about her. "I have . . . There is . . . That would be scandalous."

Yes. But the result would propel her into his arms and out of the *ton's* reach. "As they say at the Lyon's Den, there is no time like the present to make good on a bet."

"What do you know about the Lyon's Den?" Her brows furrowed, dancing across her forehead with an agility that amazed him as she grappled with uncertainty, probably mulling over propriety and other social guidelines. She glanced up and down the path. Hayden's melody diminished in the distance before another verse crescendoed. Her hand rose to her neck. "Have you gone there?"

Not in the way she imagined. "I have business with Mrs. Dove-Lyon."

"What business?" she asked in a broken whisper, the shock of such an association evident in her stare.

"Concerning the Marbles."

"The Marbles." She forced a smile. "Has the widow seen them?"

Panic rioted within him. The Lyon's Den was not a suitable topic for a lady. "I cannot say."

"Cannot or will not?"

"Her connections to Lord Elgin, and various other people of my acquaintance in the field of antiquities, are essential." Several people passed, their laughter and gaiety oppressive. "There is nothing else to say." Which was the truth.

"And despite the scandalous nature of your prize, you still intend to claim it?"

He searched the perimeter, ensuring they were alone. "I do."

She exhaled; her agitation obvious. "A kiss."

His amusement died in the presence of such gravity. His kisses had never been a disappointment before. "Yes."

"Just one?"

Hoping to reassure her, he grabbed her trembling hand. He wasn't a devil intent on stealing her virtue. It was just . . . "One kiss."

"Erm. Very well. Just one." She closed her eyes and pursed her lips, her frosty submission rubbing him the wrong way.

He wanted to kiss the woman, not fashion a martyr or anger Hera, for crying out loud.

"Open your eyes." He wasn't without feeling, and he would not take advantage of an unwilling woman. "I want you to enjoy this as much as I do."

"But how am I supposed to do that?" Her thick lashes fluttered open, revealing her enchanting blue eyes, transfixing him, trapping him, luring him into making mistakes that had consequences. When next she spoke, the truth, at last, nearly brought him to his knees. "I have never been kissed before."

His breath caught in his throat and he struggled to swallow, a sense of euphoria taking hold. "You see how easy it is to play this game?" He cupped her face, putting everything about this moment to memory. "And now, allow me to show you there are some games a man doesn't mind losing."

Pressure built in his brain and his groin. She sighed as he drew her to him, his head and manhood fighting for dominance. He pressed his mouth to hers, a tender melding of two souls, slowly increasing the pressure as Thenie allowed, fighting to remember their intimacy might be witnessed.

A part of him longed for it, yearned to mark her as his own forever.

She leaned into him, giving him permission to taste her tongue, her mouth, her lips, to keep on going without end—

Gravel crunched further down the walk, alerting them they were no longer alone. Her moan righted his thoughts. He quickly stepped back, struggling for control, at odds with himself. He quickly wiped her lips with the end of his thumb, smiled, then placed her hand on his forearm, escorting her back to the gazebo, where he'd last seen the Greys.

Music drifted on the crisp night air; the Walk illuminated by the invention of glittering light, turning night into day. Couples darted in and out of the gardens, their activities unknown, their delight undeniable. Retracing their steps, Spencer chastised himself for introducing Thenie to his morbid game. Nevertheless, he did not regret it.

Miss Parthenia Steere was everything he'd hoped she'd be.

And yet, one thing had the power to impede his courtship—she refused to tell the truth. Why? The Greys had never given him the impression she was a liar. What was she hiding? If she had never been kissed, what had really happened in Mrs. Beaumont's library?

A shadow of alarm crossed her face. "Is that—"

"The Greys?" he finished for her, gazing down at the graceful lines of her neck and longing to trail kisses all the way to the delectable mound above her closely-fitted stays. "Yes."

"No." She chewed her bottom lip and stole a look at him. "Not my cousins. Who is that person with them, the one standing in the shadows?"

CHAPTER NINE

Advices from the upper end of Piccadilly say that Mayfair lost another daughter to folly and vice. Venus and Cupid went on foot to Greenwich; Mars got drunk in Town, and Ares was set at liberty. The melancholiest part of all, was, that virtuous Diana lost her bid for freedom, an assassination of the rankest venom. The tips of savage squibs reveal she was taken in the act of fornication on the Grand Walk at Vauxhall. In this instance, even the Black Widow of Whitehall may not have the resources to save her.

—The Morning Post

"Y E MUSTN'T DO this. I beg ye. Turn back, Miss. There is still time."

Thenie didn't appreciate Clara's frankness. This was not the time to be reminded that she'd crossed the line—again—by enlisting the help of Lottie's lady's maid. She had always been a proper young woman, until Boothe's betrayal at Mrs. Beaumont's ball. Nevertheless, she had no one to blame but herself for kissing Mr. Wright-Smythe at Vauxhall. That tittle-tattle she deserved. "I am well aware of the danger. But you are the only one I can trust, Clara. Please, do not be cross."

"Ye do not trust, milady? Is she not like a sister to ye?"

She reached for Clara's hand, reassuringly. "No one, not even my cousin, can know that I asked you to chaperon me *here*, of all places."

"Commanded."

"Goodness. I did not command you. I do not have that authority." She gave in, feeling the weight of her decision. "I . . . begged."

Clara narrowed her eyes. "In either case, milady will not be happy."

Thenie released Clara's hand and clenched her own until her nails pinched the delicate tissue on her palms. "I am trying to forestall my sisters' misfortunes. And she does not have to know."

"I warn ye, she will find out."

"Not if you do not tell her." Thenie floundered like a fish out of water as she scrutinized the candlelit windows, the jovial sounds of music and laughter inviting ne'er-do-wells from every echelon of Society to enter within the doors on Cleveland Row. As they waited for the perfect moment for her to approach them, several well-dressed men advanced to the side door, and were greeted by a large man before being offered admission.

Blunt, and a determination to do anything to pursue it, was all one required to pass the door guard—Titan, was it?—therefore gaining access to the sphere of the wicked and wild, the unraveled and unprincipled.

For some strange reason she had yet to understand, her parents had always spoken highly of the Black Widow of Whitehall, though mostly shying away from the topic of the Lyon's Den, especially when her uncle was present.

According to her uncle, *'Mrs. Dove-Lyon is the type of woman who casts golden rays of hope, turning faults into assets and petitions into good fortune.'* And, *'I have been told the widow has connections in every area of Society—including former sailors and militiamen who track down runaways and couples who dash off to places unknown like Gretna Green. At worst case, should you desire it, we could take my friend's advice and seek her help.'*

Gossipmongers didn't paint the same picture of the widow, however. They cast aspersions on the stern owner said to have turned

Lyon's Gate Manor into a world of vise and vigor. But a woman who set great store by veterans and damaged people, treating them equally, and with kindness, and providing them a second chance no other would dare, could not be completely bad. Could she? It was also said that she had a certain gift, catering to those in need of matchmaking. And so, equipped with purpose and bridled with determination, Thenie had decided that acquiring the right husbands for her sisters before her reputation ruined their chances for a good match was the least she could do to make up for her rash actions.

"You will not inform my parents, Clara." Grief and despair tore at her heart. What would Mama and Papa think of her actions? What choices did she have? She felt like Odysseus, forced between a treacherous whirlpool like the one in Charybdis, and Scylla, a cliff-dwelling monster from Homer's Odyssey. Neither choice appealed. "You are my only hope."

"I suppose this isn't the first time my employer required such assistance." Clara's voice drifted off to a whisper. "Nor the last, I wager."

"What do you mean—the first time or the last?" A gamut of perplexing emotions took hold. Pulse pounding, she fought to steady her heart. Who could she possibly mean? "Have you been here before?"

Clara shook her head, deeply agitated. "I refuse to say more."

She was certainly loyal, Thenie had to give her that. Who was she protecting? Lottie? That was the only logical conclusion. But why would Lottie need the Black Widow's help? Did her decision to venture to the Lyon's Den have anything to do with the threatening letters she'd received before her marriage to Grey? If so, that provided her hope. Lottie's dilemma had come to a satisfying end.

Heaven knew that if calamity befell Thenie, it would also tarnish her father's viscountcy and her uncle's work at the British Museum, not to mention her mother, sisters, and by association, Lottie and Grey. She and Lottie had been raised from infancy together. She would go to her grave before severing that delicate bond. But conviction is what fortified the choice she'd made to travel to Whitehall. And a lady could not travel to a den of inequity alone.

Saints preserve her, she should not have come at all!

She shifted positions, adjusting the high collar of the wool garment she wore. The dull fabric felt scratchy and worn against her skin. Clara impatiently brushed her hand aside. "Do not act like this garb is foreign to ye. Ye mustn't be recognized in a place like this." Her fingers made light work of tightening the bow under her bonnet. "This tawdry gown has a purpose as old as the sun. Keep yer head down. Do not look anyone in the eye. Speak only when spoken to, and ye'll get by just fine."

"You sound as if you've done this before."

"We are not cut from the same cloth, ye and me." Clara sighed; the sound pitiful and soulless in the dark carriage. "Trust me when I say, I'm content with my lot. Ye must act like ye are too. When this is all over, ye will thank me for the momentary discomfort."

"You will wait here for me?"

She nodded. "But what if ye do not . . . come back?" Clara asked numbly, a tinge of fright lacing her voice. "What will I tell—"

"I *will* be back." If Lottie could do this, Thenie could too. Though her brain was in a tumult, and fear raged within her, her love for her sisters superseded any qualms about her questionable plan. She would go into the Lyon's Den, seek an audience with Mrs. Bessie Dove-Lyon, and remedy their plight. "I will be back," she repeated. "No harm will come to either of us."

"Ye cannot be sure."

"Did my uncle know he would find the most intact statue of Herakles when he started digging at Hadrian's Villa? When he first met Thomas Young, was he aware it would take nearly four years to decipher the Rosetta Stone and still require further study?" When Clara didn't respond, she continued. "Did my cousin ever think she'd see Grey again?" That purposeful question hit the target and Clara relaxed, ever-so-slightly. "We never know what we are capable of until we try."

Clara shook her head in dismay. "I will say a prayer for ye."

"Good." She patted the maid's hand, determined to muster on. Was she being too impulsive? Yes. But *The Flying Post*, *The Morning Post*, and *The Morning Chronicle* published editorials about ruined ladies every day. Readers speculated on the names, changed to thinly veil the actual players but done in such a way that the public would share and eventually decipher the code.

Days of blamelessness were over, whether she married or not. She'd been caught at Mrs. Beaumont's ball expressing her concerns about kissing a man. Then she *had* kissed Wright-Smythe before all and sundry on the Grand Walk. *A delightful experience it was too.*

No. Her fate was set. She did not fear for herself—not anymore. Rather, her despair centered on those she loved most dearly.

She had many regrets. In her selfishness, she had sacrificed marriage to a boorish man and chosen to play a foolish game out of boredom with a man she barely knew. She deserved what befell her, but her sisters . . . No. They were innocent. They deserved pleasure, passion, and peace. And if she could have a hand in supplying it, she would. Even debasing herself by seeking out the widow's services.

Carriage wheels rattled across the cobblestones, horses' hooves fusing with the cadence. When the street quieted, Thenie peered out the window and stared at the blue building on Cleveland Row.

"Wish me luck," she said opening the door and descending the steps.

"Good luck."

Warily, she nodded to Clara, taking comfort in the rapport they shared before turning to face the opposite side of the street. She crossed the distance, hardly breathing at all for fear she would put a foot wrong. When she arrived at the door, she knocked as she'd seen the others do.

The portal opened. There, filling the doorway, a tall, broad man looked her up and down. "Are you, Titan?" she asked.

His fierce stare bore into her. "Do I know you?"

"N-No," she said, hating the way she stammered. But, she supposed, nervousness served a purpose. "I-I would like to speak to your madam."

"She is indisposed," he said sternly, moving to shut the door. "Come back tomorrow."

"You do not understand." She stepped forward, inserting herself over the threshold in the most unladylike fashion. "I must see her tonight."

He looked her over, a frown tugging his battered face as if something about her disturbed him. *It is probably the foul-fitting wool.* "It's like that, is it?"

The look was there, compassion and condemnation, and she shivered to think of the things he'd seen and heard and been forced to do all in the name of the Black Widow of Whitehall.

She nodded, unable to speak, hoping her inability to form words improved her odds of earning his pity.

"Very well." He led her indoors, the revelry crisp and clear. People darted in and out of rooms, prominent laughter abounded, music, and other sounds like muffled thumps and gyrations taking form. "Follow me."

He led her up a long staircase to a landing. There, another man guarded an ornate door. No words were spoken between the two men, but an undercurrent of understanding passed between them because the second man motioned her closer. Boisterous laughter echoed about her, pressing her through an anteroom and into what she could only assume was the widow's office. Bookshelves lined the wall. A clock gonged. Expensive lamps illuminated the space. A rose-patterned tea set occupied a tea trolley laden with delectable sweets, the aroma mixing with the ever-present odor of tobacco marking the furniture and walls.

She approached the large mahogany desk, fearful of what she'd discover during her encounter. Would she find the helpmate her sisters required or a reluctant judge of character? Tales of the infamous widow hailed one thing about Mrs. Dove-Lyon above all others—she was a champion of the female sex.

And to her kind heart, I will make my appeal.

In the meantime, Thenie continued to peruse the room, noting the elegant style and taste presented. But it was the small painting of a model reclining in all her womanhood that caught her eye. Enthralled, she examined the size and substance of the image, and the daring it had taken to pose before a master, the artful strokes reminding her of Venice by Tecian, a painting she'd seen many times in the British Museum. She stilled, aflush with an odd tingling. The model's nude figure portrayed passion and desire. The positioning of the hands, the sensuality and beauty, the glorified fabric and flesh, was erotic and bold. She swallowed back her alarm, filled with embarrassment.

The model reminded her of someone—

Good heavens! What if the widow saw her ogling the painting?

I should not be here. Look how far I have fallen!

"Do you like it?"

She started, jumping with fright as a black clad creature emerged from the depths of the office, her movements somewhat similar to the figure she'd seen meeting Lottie and Grey at Vauxhall. But that didn't make sense. Why would her cousins be meeting the widow there?

"Come. Come. Don't be coy. I asked you a question. Do you like it?" Shock shot through her. The Black Widow of Whitehall was a tall woman, slender, her face and hands hidden, the same proportions as the woman in—

"The portrait?" Her voice squeaked an embarrassing pitch. Tempted to spin on her heels and flee the room after encountering such an intimidating female, she stole another look at the painting, her sisters' opportunities flushed to the Thames in an instant. "It is—"

"It is a cherished piece," Mrs. Dove-Lyon said. "Apropos for a place like this, do you not think?"

"I . . . do not have an opinion on the matter."

"You have eyes to see, and an adventurous spirit, if I do not miss my guess. Surely you can put what you see into words."

"It is . . . superb—the strokes intimate and complex." Revealing. "Familiar even." She bent to see the image more clearly, longing to pull the portrait from its place in the semi-darkness to inspect it further, a nagging suspicion she'd seen that person before. "Why, the woman reclining there looks very much like—"

"No one you have ever known, undoubtedly," the widow cut in. "Women like us do not run in the same circles."

Doubts niggled at her and her curiosity ran unchecked. "Do you know the artist?"

"I used to."

An abrupt sound drew their attention to the anteroom.

Suddenly, a man stood in the doorway, his posture warning he harbored unrestrained agitation, familiar, yet foreboding. "I came as soon as I heard."

"She does *not* belong here, Frost. Take her home, immediately."

Her breath caught. Surely the widow did not address Peregrine Frost. The man Lottie had hired to stop her father's blackmailer. If Mrs. Dove-Lyon refused to help her, could Frost assist her?

"Don't just stand there. Get her out of here," the widow commanded brazenly. "This is not the place for a Steere."

Her mouth dropped open and her eyes widened with horror. How was it possible that the widow knew her surname? She had not introduced herself yet. And if the widow knew who she was, would she publicize the fact that she'd been there?

"But I . . ." She'd come all this way, donned scratchy old wool, broken her parents' trust, and forced Lottie's lady's maid to accompany her. She could not leave without obtaining a contract from Mrs. Dove-Lyon that would benefit her sisters. "I would not be here if I did not need your help. I beg you. Please. Do not send me away."

"You would do best to remember your station, Miss Steere." The dark clothed creature moved stealthily to the tea service. "Time is running out, Frost. Follow my orders to the letter or you will regret it."

"Aye, madam," he said, approaching Thenie and gently taking her by the arm. He led her to the anteroom door. "Keep walking. Do not say a word."

She shot a look back over her shoulder, ignoring Frost. "I was not finished. I will not leave until I get what I came for."

"I understand. And that is why you *must* go," the widow said before the other guard shut the door behind them.

Their footsteps echoed on the staircase as they made their way hastily to the exit where Titan stood, his arms crisscrossed over his chest. He opened the door to the street beyond.

"What are you doing here?" Frost asked as he escorted her to her carriage. There, seated alone, a very distressed Clara anxiously waited. "You are not supposed to be here."

"Take your hands off me," she ordered. Her hat fell askew as she struggled. She snatched her arm away but found herself equally ensnared by Frost's strong grip. He carried her off, roughly loading her into the carriage. "I am capable of taking care of myself."

"I have heard that line before." Frost entered the coach and sat across from her, easing himself onto the squabs. "Miss Steere, it is not you that I am concerned about, but how your cousin will deal with me if she finds out what you have done."

"My cousin?" Thenie drew back to study the muscular blond man. "You have helped my cousin before, have you not?" In her struggle to see him in the dimly lit interior, she knocked off his glasses. He quickly righted them and jerked down his hat before she had the opportunity to fully view his face. The man's threadbare attire belied his gentlemanly manners, offering no clue as to his true station. But his scent—tobacco and cedar—held sway. *Grey?* Good God, no! It could not be.

Why, in heaven's name, would her cousin's husband disguise himself in such a manner? And why would he be at the Lyon's Den? "Are you—"

"Peregrine Frost, at your service," he confirmed without validating her suspicions. "I see you have coerced your cousin's lady's maid into helping you."

Clara shifted on the squabs. "I offered me services."

"You are a dear for covering for me, Clara, but I will not allow you to be punished for my choices." She turned her attention to Frost. "I *made* her accompany me."

"Do you realize what could have happened to both of you?" Frost produced a pistol, leveling it at the window as if expecting trouble. "Cleveland Row is not for virtuous females." He glared at Clara from across the carriage. "You, of all people, should know this. If I hadn't been nearby . . ." He shook his head, the action making his poorly tied cravat scrape his sideburns—a sign of masculinity and power. "This is not what I expected, and I am at a loss for words. I must get you back to where you belong without further harm to your reputation."

"Pfft." She swallowed back a sob, desperately wanting to claw the man's eyes out. "I fear it is already too late for that." Frustrated that Mrs. Dove-Lyon had ordered him to escort her out of the Lyon's Den, and alarmed by the presence of the investigator who knew so much about Lottie and condemned her so readily, she fought to keep her spirits in check. If this was Grey, his concealment heightened her disgrace. "This was my only chance to make things right, and you have ruined it."

"I have everything under control. Leave the particulars to me. Mother Abbess is not immune to the pleas of innocent women."

"Mother Abbess?" she asked, stupefied.

"The Black Widow of Whitehall."

Clara grabbed Thenie's hand. "Ye saw her?"

"Never speak of the Lyon's Den. From this moment forward, the gaming hell's name should never leave your lips. If you had stayed at the Lyon's Den any longer—" Frost tapped on the ceiling. The equipage groaned, and the vehicle lunged into motion. "You might very well have ended up an opportunist's prize, or carried off to Gretna Green to settle a debt. Is that the legacy you want to leave your sisters?"

"How dare you!" She lunged forward in an effort to slap him. "You have no right to mention my sisters."

He seized her wrist. "I have more right than you know. And be warned, I do not take my obligations lightly."

"What do you mean?" She was tired of his banter, his holier than thou attitude, and covert claims.

"Deep down, you know."

I certainly do not. Though she suspected Grey operated in covert and nefarious dealings, she was not willing to disclose her discovery— yet. Clara was present, and if he required secrecy, a servant was the least likely person to keep it. So, rather than falsely accuse the man of trickery, she'd wait to speak to her cousin "I just want to protect my family."

"If that is the case, I suggest you look closer to home."

She grasped Clara's hand, requiring her support, her heart and mind at war. Frost had done investigatory work for Lottie, coming to her cousin's aid at a time when Lottie thought her world would implode. If Thenie's suspicions were correct—that Frost was Grey— he'd originally disguised himself to get back into Lottie's life. But why continue the charade after their marriage? She could think of no reason for him to have an alliance with Mrs. Bessie Dove-Lyon. What reason did he have for being at the Lyon's Den?

"You are persistent," she said. "I give you that much. Very well. I shall seek my cousin's help. Maybe she can shed light on the reasons you feel it's your duty to protect me."

"Seek the truth, and you will find it," he said.

But would she like what she discovered?

CHAPTER TEN

Frank Careless, as soon as his valet has helped on and adjusted his clothes, goes to his glass and tumbles his cravat; in short, undressing himself to go into company. Will Nice is so little satisfied, that all the time he is more insufferable, because he is careless. Cressida is distracted. Whom to pursue? Will is every way so careful, that she fears his length of days. Frank is so loose, that she fears for her own health with him. Careless is a coxcomb, and Nice a fop; two hopeful candidates for a woman set at liberty. But there is a whisper, she will be given to Tom Terror the gamester whose habit of undoing women ensures that he'll certainly succeed if introduced; for nothing so much prevails with the vain part of that sex, as the glory of deceiving them who have deceived others.

—The Morning Post

THE NEXT DAY, due to their late return to the townhouse through a back servant's entrance in the Mews, Thenie did not rise until mid-morning. She opened her eyes and shuddered, pulling a pillow over her face as the sun, in all its brilliance, invaded the fleeting peace sleep had provided. The soft footfalls of her maid, Tilly, resounded somewhere in the room, hinting the day was well under way, and only a fool squandered an opportunity to make use of it.

She rose with a start, blood draining from her face. Instantly chilled, she suddenly remembered she needed to speak to her cousin, and without delay.

Peregrine Frost!

"Are ye unwell, Miss?" A small, stout, brunette with a silver streak oddly placed to the right of her forehead, Tilly rushed to her side in a fever of concern, nearly tripping over her skirts to reach her. While Tilly wasn't as well-balanced or lithe as Clara, her devotion to Thenie was unmatched.

She shot out her hand to stave off Tilly's advance. "I am not going to be sick."

"Ye're as white as the mantel. I thought—"

"Do not distress yourself." She peered at the windows, wondering what Lottie and her sisters were doing at this hour. Would they be reading the scandal sheets? *The Morning Post* arrived on Tuesdays. "I am well. Truly. What time is it?"

"Half past eleven." Past time for the *Post.* Tilly worked diligently to fluff up the pillows behind Thenie's head so that she could lean back and adapt to being awake. "I shall 'ave Cook send up a tray while I select garments fer the day."

"You needn't bother. I shall break my fast with the rest of the family."

Tilly went still. "The family has already broken their fast."

"Already?" she asked, shaken.

"Yer father and his brother went to the museum. Lord Grey took Mr. Wright-Smythe to meet Lord Elgin. Yer sisters are makin' their mornin' visits, and yer mother is attendin' one of 'er philan—"

"Thropic." At Tilly's questionable stare, she repeated, "Philan-thropic."

"Aye. That. She is at one of 'er meetin's."

"That leaves Lottie. Is she still in residence?"

Tilly's grin lit up the room. "Oh, yes, Miss. She is at 'er leisure in the library, readin'."

She sighed happily. At least that was something. Her family's schedule benefited her. Now, she could have a guarded conversation with her cousin about Grey and Peregrine Frost. "Thank you. As it turns out, I *would* like a tray. Can you send a message to the kitchen?"

Bobbing a curtsy, Tilly said, "Right away, miss."

Hours later, wearing a purple muslin gown, Tilly had meticulously ironed, Thenie made her way downstairs. Her mind was troubled but her spirits soared. She was dressed in her favorite garment, the lavender overlay made of delicate gossamer matched her slippers and the ribbons in her hair. And she knew exactly where to find her cousin—Papa's library, where Lottie enjoyed reading extensively.

Arriving there, she lent her ear to the door, hearing nothing from the interior but an occasional clatter of horses' hooves echoing from the street below. She turned the latch and entered her father's inner sanctum. There, her cousin sat in one of the bow windows, her knees tucked beneath her on the cushions, a book of antiquities lifted practically up to her nose.

She glanced up, adjusting the rim of her glasses. "Oh, there you are. I had almost given up hope you would ever appear and was beginning to think there might be something wrong. Tilly assured me you were quite well, however."

She patted the window seat, indicating she wanted Thenie to join her.

"She is all well and good." Thenie quietly closed the door then made her way to her cousin's side. But she did not sit down. This conversation would not be an easy one. "To be frank, however, I did not sleep well."

"I heard." Her cousin's smart response took Thenie off-guard. At her startled expression, Lottie raised her hand to set her at ease. "Clara told me." *Clara.* She'd forgotten the maid would confide in her cousin. Despair sank in. "Do not scold her. She and I have been through so much together that there is little she will not unburden herself of. And in this instance, your welfare was her primary concern."

Where to start? *With an apology.* "I—"

"Thenie, what were you thinking?" Shocked by her cousin's abrupt attack, she took a few steps back as Lottie placed the book on the sill and reached for her hand. "To the Lyon's Den, of all places? If you needed anything, you know that Septimus and I would labor to get it for you without question." She shook her head, gloomily. "We have overcome tricky situations before, but to put yourself in danger that way . . ." *Good God!* Was Lottie as horrified as Thenie felt listening to her describe her antics? "There are other ways to combat problems." She turned back to her, the tears glistening in her eyes threatening to escape. "Other ways more constructive and cautious. What if you had been seen there? What if—"

"I know. I know." Lottie's revulsion left a sour taste in Thenie's mouth. "I made a horrible mistake."

"Did you consider what could have happened to Clara if you were caught?"

They *were* caught . . . and by Peregrine Frost. "I left her in the carriage, guarded by the driver. She was safe there."

"And no one has ever been accosted in a carriage before?" Her statement bruised Thenie's pride. "Certainly, not anyone on Cleveland Row?"

"I am sorry," she said accosted by a severe case of misery as she rushed into Lottie's embrace. "I was desperate. I—"

"Chose not to confide in me." Lottie's words cut through her soul, the wound festering into a deadly mix. She was right, though there had been few moments of privacy between them since her cousin's arrival.

The damn burst. She sobbed, unable to control herself as passion and poison poured from every fiber of her being. In seeking a love like Lottie's and Grey's, she had inadvertently destroyed her sisters' prospects and tainted every aspect of her cousins' return.

What must Lottie think of her? "Things are not . . . what they seem."

"Is that so?" Lottie asked. "From where I sit, it appears that *you* have only yourself to blame for your troubles, which is so unlike you. What will those who love you think? Are you so unwilling to divulge the truth, that you would jeopardize your relationship with your family, with us, with Wright-Smythe?" A knot twisted in the pit of her stomach. "Has something happened? Has Wright-Smythe offended you in some way?"

She clasped her hands, wringing them nervously. "No."

"Thenie." Lottie tsked. "Never, in all my wildest dreams, would I have imagined that you would keep secrets between us."

If you only knew. "When you and Grey married," she explained, "I was over the moon, filled with a happiness and hope that I could not have properly bestowed on anyone else. You were meant for each other, you and Grey, bound by affection and adoration, seasons and space. I thought . . . well, I feared that I should never see the like of it ever again. And, I am ashamed to admit, I was jealous, desiring the same type of experience myself." She collected her emotions, making a sad attempt at drying her eyes with the back of her hand. "I did something stupid. Something I have regretted for nigh onto a week."

"What did you do, Thenie?" Lottie narrowed her gaze, but her countenance remained friendly and open. "Surely the stakes are not as drastic as they seem."

"They are worse." A wave of apprehension swept through her. She swallowed hard, lifted her chin, and boldly met her cousin's stare. "Prepare yourself."

"Go on." Lottie reached out and squeezed her hand, reassuringly. "I am listening."

Her pulse beat erratically, walls of deceit and discouragement crumbling down. "I-I refused Lord Boothe."

"I know." Lottie had undoubtedly heard the rumors, of course.

Her unemotional reaction was perplexing, however. "Why?"

"Well . . ." She was tired of lying to her parents and sisters, tired of fighting with all her might to keep from admitting the truth to Wright-Smythe, and to herself. "I do not love him."

"But I thought—" Lottie corrected herself abruptly. "The two of you seemed well-suited the last time I saw you together."

"Yes. I did fancy myself smitten with him for a time. His stoicism and betrayal staged the final blow, however." She turned and began slowly pacing. "He is a good man, but I cannot marry without love. Not after." She covered her face, fighting back the tears that still threatened to flow. "Especially after seeing the way Grey looks at you."

"Is that all?" Her cousin's embrace was immediate.

Dumbfounded, she asked, "All?"

"Boothe will move on. Men like him always do. He is wealthy and good-looking, with a brilliant career ahead of him. Someone worthy will catch his eye." Lottie rose from the windowsill to embrace her fully. "And you—my dear sister, given your sweet and loving nature—will find a man to love you with all his heart. Perhaps," she said, drawing out the word, "you have already met him?"

"Perhaps." If Lottie implied Wright-Smythe. Her heart pounded madly every time she thought of him, and the kiss they shared. Partial to his energy and power, she shrugged dismissively. Love had no place in her life if her sisters were forced to marry for convenience because of her past mistakes. "Even if I have, there is another reason for my shame."

Lottie leaned back, studying her face. "Go on."

"There is an assassination of character in progress. Someone—I suspect within Boothe's circle or perhaps Boothe himself—has venomously spread gossip about my presence at Mrs. Beaumont's ball. What was merely supposition has been spun as fact, the threads cobwebbing into the minds of tattlers and even now, infiltrating events of the season."

"It is so unlike you to be careless, Thenie. You are always proper. What could you have possibly said that would warrant such a disgrace?"

"My life will not be ruined by a kiss."

Lottie laughed, the sound annoying Thenie's already frayed nerves.

"This is serious."

"Is Lord Boothe's kiss repulsive?" Lottie squeezed her shoulder as if to shake some sense into her. "Is that why you dread what your dismissal of his intentions might do to your reputation? You fear he will retaliate?"

"I suspect he already has." She shook her head, crisscrossing her arms. "I found myself needing air. I went into Mr. Beaumont's library and began reading Hamlet aloud. That led to a debate of whether kissing a stranger would help me to know how to kiss Boothe without him being the wiser that I did not love him. I had never been kissed before and had no idea how it was done."

"Had?" Lottie quickly picked up on the slip of her tongue. "Nevermind that now," she reassured her. "Conversations are overheard all the time and taken out of context. The *ton* knows this. But its hunger for the vulgar slander of others oftentimes raises false flags which reflect badly on those who initiated the scurrilous details."

"But my sisters," she pleaded. "What is to become of them?"

"I see." The beginning of a smile curved Lottie's lips. "Your female heart set out on a reckless raid, like those you frequently preached against when we were young. But by going to the Black Widow of Whitehall—"

"Yes, but," she had no reason to deny the truth now, "that investigator you hired—Peregrine Frost? He prevented me from requesting Mrs. Dove-Lyon's help."

"I feel I must ask you why you thought the widow could help

Augusta and Delphi. Why not, your mother and father? Or me?"

She stopped pacing and slowly turned in a circle to face her cousin. "I was, am, ashamed. I mentioned Mrs. Beaumont's ball, but I failed to mention that I kissed Mr. Wright-Smythe at Vauxhall."

"The two of you . . . at Vauxhall?" Lottie's mood brightened. "And?"

"Lottie! We were seen. My reputation is ruined, and by proxy, my sisters'."

"Nonsense." She allowed her cousin to lead her to a leather settee, where they could sit face to face, hoping Lottie was right, but anticipating the worst. "Let's shelve that conversation for a moment and go back to your escapade to Cleveland Row. It is fortunate for all of us that Frost was at the Lyon's Den at the time. His presence prevented you from making a very big mistake."

"I knew what I was doing." She hated the bitter tone in her voice, especially the weakness that made her legs shake beneath her skirts. "He foiled my plans."

"What plans? Did you expect to auction your sisters off at the gaming tables?"

She clenched her jaw to curtail the sob threatening to burst from her throat. "Certainly not." Her cousin's disapproval stung. "I would not do that to Augusta and Delphi."

"And I would not cause any of you harm. Extend the same consideration to me, will you? Do not judge Frost too harshly. If you love me as you say you do, please do not dislike him overmuch," she said softly. "You see, Peregrine Frost has a special place in my heart. He is important to me. He's a part of this family and has invested a great deal in securing our safety."

"What do you mean, he is a part of this family?" she asked, blinking with bafflement.

"I vowed to you once that I would do anything for those I love." Lottie rose in one fluid motion and raised her chin, defiantly. "Peregrine Frost is my husband."

"What?" Thenie bolted to her feet as her cousin's admission cut through her. "But how? When?"

"Septimus *is* Peregrine Frost," she said, cupping Thenie's chin to gaze into her upturned face. "It seems inconceivable to you, I am sure, but it is true."

"But you hired Frost."

"I did," she explained. "They are one and the same, Thenie. After Septimus left Cambridge, he joined the Admiralty, where his proficiency in antiquities led him to counterintelligence. He then returned to England when his father unexpectedly died to accept the barony. But, unused to a static lifestyle, he ached to test investigatory skills he employed on the continent. There was only one way to do that without being recognized. He had to change his name, disguise himself and his station. Ultimately, Mrs. Bessie Dove-Lyon sought his services."

Anxiety yielded to bewilderment. "He works for *her*."

"He does," Lottie said. "But there's more."

Saints preserve her. She'd counted herself an excellent sleuth in the carriage with Frost, but she hesitated to hazard a guess as to what Lottie implied. "More?"

"Do sit down." Lottie guided her back to the settee and smiled warmly. "Prepare yourself. *She* is my mother."

"Your—" Thenie swallowed tightly, unable to process what she'd just heard. "But your mother died the day you were born."

Lottie shook her head. "She pretended to, for my sake."

The idea was so absurd, she rejected it. "I do not understand."

"You will." Her cousin's dark brown gaze probed her very soul. "Trust me."

Thenie scavenged her memories to reinforce her cousin's claims. Anger boiled inside her. This lie affected everything, everyone. Their childhood, their sisterhood, their adulthood. Nothing made sense. "I am . . . speechless," she said, her mind spinning in circles that came round and round to the same conclusion.

Nothing was as it seemed. While she and Wright-Smythe had been playing a game, the sum of her life was a lie.

Lottie clutched her hands, drawing them up like a bridge between them. "I understand the dilemma you find yourself in. Believe me, I do. I only just learned the truth before my marriage to Septimus. And then the wedding took place and we were off on the Tour. There was no time to share this secret with you."

"How is such a thing possible? Tell me." She labored to understand the implications as nausea gripped her. "Mama knew. All. This. Time. And Papa—"

"Your father knew I was his brother's only child and little else. Bless him. He is such a good family man that he accepted me readily and without argument and treated me as if I was his own."

"That alone should be enough, I suppose." But anger raged inside her. She'd been duped by her own family. "So, *you* are the daughter of my uncle *and* the infamous matchmaker and owner of the Lyon's Den?"

"I am." Thenie's thoughts raced dramatically, every facet of her being combatting shame and blame at once. "She is nothing like the vile things you and I have heard gossipmongers say," Lottie assured her. "My mother is kind, affectionate, and cares a great deal about our welfare. So much so, that when Papa failed to return from Hadrian's Villa within a year's time, she gave me up so that I would have a proper education—a decision she claims to regret to this day."

"You believe her?" she asked, dumbfounded.

"A woman in her position needs a man's protection. Without marriage to my father, or at least his financial support, where was she to go? What was she to do?"

Thenie mulled over the answer. The chances of a courtesan's survival, when cut off by her benefactors, did not broker good odds.

Children of such women suffered excruciating hardships and hazardous ends.

A child's life should not be wagered.

"My mother took a chance by trusting your mother to do what was right. She knew my aunt had just given birth and was in a position to care for me. And my aunt assured my mother that I would be raised like her daughters, as one of the family."

"We *are* family," Thenie insisted. "And you are correct. Mama would never turn away an innocent babe."

"She did not." Thenie fought back the happy tears that threatened to spill down her cheeks. "And I am who I am today because of that kindness," Lottie said. "So, can we now put any scandal associated with our family to rest and discuss Wright-Smythe?"

"Oh, yes!" the twins said as they strode happily through the library doors.

Augusta winked at Thenie. "Is he not the most—"

"Handsome of men?" Delphi finished for her.

"I daresay he is," Lottie agreed, smiling sweetly.

She fought to stay silent, the shadows cloaking her heart dispersing. She'd learned long ago not to argue with her sentimental sisters. The irony was, in this instance, she did not want to. There was a tender side to Wright-Smythe that surpassed his infuriating arrogance. And every inch of her ached for him, shutting down her prejudices.

Truth be told, she missed their little game, having enjoyed their *tête-à-tête* immensely. The sheer hysteria of winning a kiss and the brand of its burning sweetness stayed with her, awakening the warrior within. And that challenging arousal reluctantly raced through her.

Did Wright-Smythe feel it too?

CHAPTER ELEVEN

Calista desires the sort of man who can have no greater views than what are in her power to give him. Her utmost ambition is, to be thought a woman of fashion. With artful poise, she selects a man who loves her because others do, rather than choosing one who approves of her on his own judgment. A man in love will often change his opinion; but the woman that follows the sense of others, is chastened to be constant. The visits, the diversions, and proposals, will be arguments for a man with second-hand genius. Calista, however, takes note and waits, enjoying a Season or two longer, remaining a single woman and enjoying such devotion, in the sublime pleasure of being followed and admired; which nothing can equal, except that of being persuaded and prized.

—The Morning Post

I T FELT AS if a sennight had passed since the kiss Spencer had shared with Thenie at Vauxhall and he'd been unable to think about little else since. His mind relived the moment with impromptu frequency—the intimacy and the threat of discovery, Thenie's velvety warmth, and his longing to take sweet possession of her, mastering her passions. His emotions had whirred and skidded at every encounter since; his heart thundering, his body reacting with primal need. He'd attended two balls and an intimate dinner, the details all but lost to him now. The only remembrances he treasured were the divine way Thenie had looked in her many silk gowns, her grace and gentility, the length of her neck and the delightful way her throat dipped to her bosom. His breath hitched, the prolonged anticipation of seeing her again, a challenge he'd never predicted to encounter.

Thenie, by contrast, practiced avoidance, closely guarding her defenses until her cousins intervened on his behalf. What was she afraid of? *Him?* He would never allow harm to come to her, though he was aware rumors circulated about their kiss at Vauxhall—a result of his stupidity. In the days they'd spent apart, he'd yearned to show her affection and adventure, to feed her curiosity and share antiquity's secrets. Like Athena, she was a goddess who deserved a declaration, love and devotion. What he experienced wasn't lust, but something more, and the thrill of it excited him to his core. He wanted to share every second of his life with Thenie. He longed for her companionship, the scope of his existence and all that they could discover together in the field and in each other's arms.

"Are you coming, Wright-Smythe?"

Spencer stopped in his tracks and gave Lord Steere and his brother, Professor Walcot, an affirmative nod. They'd spent the morning in the British Museum, finishing up a meeting with Lord Elgin. Or Elgin's solicitor. The wily lord had managed to avoid him again, sending the wig-toting curmudgeon to share the news.

"Don't let Elgin get to you." Walcot squeezed his shoulder. "He's just up to the same old tricks."

"I'll continue to force the issue, in your stead, Wright-Smythe," Steere said. "Believe me when I say, the museum seeks to do what is right where the Marbles are concerned."

"Meaning the powers that be will send the stones back to Athens if the firman cannot be found?" he asked.

Steere guffawed. "I have no say in that, exactly."

"My brother means," Walcot said, "England has financed Elgin's ventures for far too long to give up now, to include the costly destruction aboard the *Mentaur*."

Oh, Elgin was keen to save the Marbles, his seed idea being to decorate his home as Lansdowne and others had done. War and diplomacy and sheer luck profited the man. And according to Elgin, the Turkish government had no claim on the sculptures because it had detached their heads and pounded them to dust. And so, the sinking in 1801, off the coast of Greece had generated massive outrage, the heavy cache pulling the ship under after hitting a rock before barely leaving the harbor. The concept of *"my acquisition" "my marbles" "my property"* and *"I shall regret nothing of my acquisitions in Greece"* was criminal, in Spencer's estimations.

"The *Mentaur* carried seventeen pieces of Marbles and fourteen pieces of friezes, at an exorbitant cost of £5,000 to salvage."

Steere agreed to Spencer's calculations. "Emptying Elgin's purse and forcing him to borrow; a concept almost too catastrophic to imagine."

"A travesty dictated by haste," Spencer added without hesitancy. Elgin's plan was to get the Marbles to England before the Ottoman learned of his scheme. The man was dictated by a rage of possession, claiming tourists bribed the Turks to break off pieces of the Marbles in the 18th Century. Whatever the case, the stones were Athens' legacy, an inheritance he suspected would continue to be plucked until the past was rewritten or gone. "Elgin will be forced to sell, mark my words."

"Do you really think so?" the professor asked.

"Can the people of Athens afford them?"

Spencer glared at Steere then shook his head. "The Marbles belong in Athens whether the people can afford them or not." The Ottoman Sultan had given his permission for the removal of rubbish, making no opposition to inscribed blocks and figures Elgin found around the base of the temple. Which pieces he could pilfer were not made completely clear, unfortunately, because 'the interpretation that the rulers of Athens allowed it to bear' gave Elgin and Hunt leeway to do as they pleased. "I am not the only one who thinks this way. Byron's poem attacks Elgin, referring to him as a plunderer and villain. Is that how we want the world to view Britains?"

"Careful," Steere said, "lest you raise the riot."

The professor plucked his brother away, his expression animated. "Wright-Smythe does not oppose showing the Marbles to the public as long as it is legally done, brother. And that settles the debate between us, because the ladies have arrived."

"Papa!" Lottie exclaimed, escorted by Grey and to his right. To the left of him, Thenie was flanked by her sisters, August and Delphi. "We have arrived at last. I do hope that you have good news for us."

Spencer braced himself for a fight that did not come.

"I do," Walcot said. "An agreement has been reached and we have finally been given permission to exhibit the Rosetta Stone to academics far and wide. Do follow me, please. Young and I have a little celebration planned and wish to share the particulars with you all."

Would Lord Steere take the bait? He had already declared that Thenie should not view the carnal marvels, and Spencer agreed that Miss Augusta and Miss Delphi should not view the Marbles—yet.

He held his breath as Walcot led the Steeres to the upper rooms.

The Grey's held back, his friend raising his elbow for Lottie to grab hold. She laid her hand on his forearm and said softly, "Do not let this opportunity go to waste."

Spencer bowed his head, thanking them for allowing him this time to speak with Thenie alone. Given space, he meant to introduce Thenie to the brazen world of the Athenians in Elgin's room.

Standing side by side, Spencer waited expectantly for Thenie to acknowledge him as she watched her cousins depart. She trained her vision on anything but him in the great hall on the second floor, eluding his stare, making him wonder if she had second thoughts and had decided against accepting his invitation to see the Marbles. Then, a breathless euphoria took hold as she looked his way, an impish gleam in her eyes. She was a vision, standing in quiet surrender, as curious about his intentions as he was about what her reaction might be.

He raked his gaze over her slowly, aware of the many museum visitors roaming about and what they might think of his behavior. He longed to draw her into his arms. But thankfully, he had more sense than that, at least in the open where everyone could see. "You have accepted my dare."

"Yes," she said turning to stare back at him, her beautiful, delectable mouth thinning. "The opportunity was . . . too electrifying to ignore."

The smoldering flame dancing in her eyes had a startling effect on him. Did she feel it too? He didn't have time to ask as she pretended to examine a bust of Marcus Aurelius. She walked to the statue, her fingers skimming the Grecian lines and making him wonder how her hands would feel exploring his skin.

"Do you enjoy sketching?" she asked, apparently having noted the large book he carried. A rush of blood shot through his veins, the invigorating pleasure having nothing to do with reason. "Would a man of . . . your talents be willing to show his drawings to an amateur?"

Astonished by her interest in his work, he said, "All you need to do is ask."

"May I?" She held out her hand, providing him a closer look at her lacy gloves—creamy confections that cobwebbed over her skin.

"Of course." He handed her his drawings, a bout of unease wrapping around his gut. He had nothing to hide, but would her opinion of him change when she viewed the nudes?

Thenie opened the book and perused his illustrations, page after page, her eyes widening, fingers pausing here and there, stroking lines, her gaze darting up to his and locking on with curiosity and surprise.

"These are . . ." She closed the book—her eyes, her mouth—straightening the binding before handing it back to him and glancing around as if to make sure no one observed the interaction. "You have a steady hand."

He preferred the term, *practiced*. "I have a practiced hand. Artists must be persistent."

"As Pericles was, I am sure." She pointed to the bust of Marcus Aurelius. "Do you think this is a good likeness?"

"Of Marcus Aurelius?" At her nod, he said, "What astounds me is this bust is still in one piece—unlike the Marbles."

"How long, do you suppose, did subjects have to sit for statues like this?"

"To my knowledge, models were sketched first, the renderings later converted to paintings or sculptures, the choice dependent on the master."

"Do you ever stop to wonder," she asked, tilting her head as she studied the piece, "if Socrates and Plato contemplated these very same relics?"

"I have." Her figure caught the light just so, illuminating the aristocratic swoop of her brow, the curve of her nose and her high cheekbones, making him desire to sketch her without worrying about proprieties or limitations Society placed on them. "I do. Though, I doubt great men like Socrates and Plato understood—or could have foreseen—the extent to which mankind would go to profit from them."

A couple crossed their path, forcing another excruciating pause in their conversation. "Simply scandalous," the man said, frowning. "Boothe is an admirable man."

"Just look at her now," his partner spat, "prancing around the museum with *him*!"

Bollocks! Spencer took a menacing step forward. That was all it took to intimidate the pair. They rushed away, complaining.

"Pay no attention to them," he said, capturing Thenie's arm and leading her away. "The antiquities market attracts ne'er-do-wells who glory in cultural superiority at every opportunity."

"Papa has said the very same thing." She studied him calmly as he escorted her down the Hall, making him wonder what occupied her mind. "You are an unusual man." Her voice drifted into a hushed whisper, a wide range of emotion—pure and unsullied—moving over her face. "I sense you do not approve of the noble asylum this museum provides for artifacts from locations all over the world, to include the wandering dead. And yet . . . you *are* here."

What is she getting at? He placed his hands behind his back and interlocked his fingers. "Housing relics facing destruction is one thing. Enabling people to venture to faraway places so they can observe those objects in their natural habitat is quite another."

"And have you seen a great deal of relics in your lifetime?"

"Too many to count."

She laughed, hardly seeming to care if anyone heard. He took this as a prompt to escort her to the wrought-iron landing. There, the staircase led to the upper floor where all things Roman and Greek and Egyptian, fossils, insects, birds, reptiles, and fish were exhibited. It was also where Walcot and Young's Rosetta Stone resided, making his tactic to slip into Elgin's room more dangerous than ever. A look below provided a spiraling view of stairs rising to landings and several sets of doors which led to other halls and rooms flanked by rare stuffed animals.

With any luck, the Greys' plan to distract the Steeres was under way.

"Your cousins enjoyed their Tour," he said to distract her, sharing information she already knew. Realizing his gaffe, he swallowed back a groan. "Would you ever consider traveling to Rome, Egypt, or Greece?"

"I *am* British." She stared at him as if he'd grown horns on his head. "We are drawn to mystery and antiquated things, are we not?"

Like a horse to water. "Are you interested in visiting the Acropolis?"

"Pfft. You heard my father. I cannot venture abroad on my own." She inhaled a quick breath. "What I mean to say is—"

"Understood. By the by, the exhibits, here, hardly compare to marveling at the real architecture you are named after, Parthenia." He searched her eyes, longing to take her to Athens and show her all, realizing too late that he'd used her Christian name. "There, columns rise heavenward, as far as the eye can see. The ancients are celebrated at the temple once a year in a ceremony to honor Athena. And above it all, metopes and friezes, molded by perception and proximity, and in mindboggling poses, watch and wait as mere mortals pay homage."

She sighed, her bosom visibly heaving. "That sounds . . . breathtaking. But you must understand. I am *no* stranger to antiquities."

"No," he agreed, the challenge in her voice making him desire to refine her education more than ever. "I see that. Nevertheless, there is no comparison to being *there*."

Spencer stretched out his arm to escort her upstairs. An enchanting smile touched Thenie's lips as she accepted his chivalrous offer, and together, they passed an exhibit of sarcophaguses on their way to his private screening. Heart beating expectantly, he wondered how she'd react to the sight of the Marbles. Would she find them disturbing or one of the most sensual objects she'd ever seen?

DETERMINED TO PROVE to herself to Wright-Smythe, Thenie vowed that nothing she saw in Elgin's room would shock her. She had much to atone for—speaking out of turn and birthing erroneous gossip, rejecting a worthy suitor, and making Clara an accessory to her crazy scheme to acquire the Black Widow of Whitehall's help. She needn't have bothered. The flaw in her plan had revealed a closely-guarded secret that—if discovered by the wrong source—could ruin them all. And then there was Wright-Smythe. She hadn't played fair with him during their foolhardy game. She'd refused to tell the truth, preferring, instead, to perform dare after dare. And now he was going to take her into Elgin's room and show her the Marbles.

Her heart lurched wildly as Wright-Smythe levered the latch leading to Elgin's cache of antiquities. The hinges complained as the door opened, the sound a portent of doom. He stepped back and motioned for her to go in first. She hesitated, tempted deeply to turn tail and run like a frightened rabbit.

Was she equipped for such a sensual sight? More dangerous, was she ready to be alone with this man in a British Museum chamber? Emboldened by the warm and inviting smile he flashed her, all sense of right and wrong vanished.

She walked right in. He followed then locked the door behind them, the clicking mechanism offering assurance that they wouldn't be disturbed by the artists and politicians who ventured to Elgin's domain to worship the Athenian treasure.

Pushing the ramifications of that act aside, she was immediately struck by the contrast of light and dark in the room, and the cold inflexibility of stone that spoke of another time, another realm. What awaited her was not what she expected. The room was filled with classical stonework slouching and stretching and straining in various poses, shapes and sizes, the definition of each carving alive in high-relief. Metopes, nearly four feet square, rose above a row of meticulously arranged friezes, a configuration of racing horses circling the room in a majestical procession. Below that, fragments of pediments were tucked in the wall, and in the center of the room stood the *magnum opus*, lounging in archaic glory.

"Dionysos." His powerful hand moved over the magnificent creature, flesh and blood contrasting with the man striving to break away from stone. "He originally looked down on Athens from the temple's Eastern facade, the pediment portraying the birth of Athena from the head of her father, Zeus."

Wright-Smythe moved around the figure, lithe and sure, a man completely in his element. She followed, mesmerized by his physicality, trying in vain to ignore the sight of the statue's manly features and the way her body reacted to both.

"Look here," he said. "Time has honeyed the iron in the marble, altering the stone's pigment." He lowered his stare to the floor, directing her attention to the placement of his foot. Nearby, the head of a horse protruded from the ground as if held by the gruesome hands of Fate, its body trapped in a horrific cage beneath. Veins traveled across its face, lifelike and surreal, giving one the impression that blood pumped within. "The horse of Selene, the moon goddess."

"Breathtaking!" It was all so spectacular.

Behind him, another section of pediment, angelic and oddly placed caught her attention.

"Ah. You like that one," he said, approaching the statue. The headless, armless figure had been fashioned by classical genius. Her *Dionysos* stroked the feather-light tunic cascading over the statue's barely-veiled nude form, the illusory fabric a wet illusion, the sight forming a tingling in the pit of her stomach and making her wish Wright-Smythe would touch her in the same way. "Hestia, goddess of the hearth. Splendor and shadow."

A cloak, draping in broader waves, fell behind Hestia to her knees. The heavy weight settling over her at the same time a wave of astonishment flooded her mind. "How did they do it?"

"Do it?" he asked, dropping his eyes to her bosom.

Good heavens! Conscious of his virile appeal, she fought to keep her mind out of the clouds. "Create such stunning works of art."

"What you see here is nothing compared to what survives of the temple itself."

She stared back at him in awe, wondering if Pericles had been visited by the heavenly realm. Sprees from mythical gods and creatures, surely. And Wright-Smythe. What of him? Why did he seem so natural in this place, like the stuff of mythic legend she'd been allowed to read about? Every movement he made far exceeded the sight of naked limbs and hard muscle. It was easy for her to imagine his rugged, tanned features, and perfectly toned body exerting bold feats of bravery and conquest.

Thenie recalled the kiss they'd shared at Vauxhall, her knees weakening with the effort, the heady sensation fresh and alive as they stood several feet apart. How had he done it? In so short a time, he'd entered her life, won over her family, challenged her at every turn, championed her spirit, and earned her respect—a respect that amplified and adapted as her physical awareness of him increased.

She tried to quiet her quickening pulse but to no effect. Being alone with him was more scandalous than practicing a kiss on a stranger, possibly ruining her sisters' futures, being discovered at the Lyon's Den, being related to the Black Widow of Whitehall, or viewing the Marbles.

A hot ache grew in her throat as he caressed the plastered folds of cloth clinging to . . . *Oh, what is happening to me. It is positively indecent to wonder what it would feel like for him to touch me that way.*

"What is the matter?" She stifled an outcry of delight, praying he couldn't read her thoughts. The heat rising to her cheeks surely gave her away. "Cat got your tongue?"

An intense understanding flared between them as he revisited the conversation from when they first met. "If you recall," she said, becoming more brazen, "I do not need a cat to warm my lap."

He backed away from the pediment, drawing closer. "I do."

A peculiar light shone in his eyes, erotic and entrancing. He placed his hands on either side of her face, gently cupping her cheeks, he lowered his head to hers. She waited until their lips were about to touch before saying, "Sir, we are no longer playing the game. You won, remember?"

He searched her soul. "Did I?" The real world outside Elgin's room ceased to exist in that moment.

"You were seen kissing me on the Grand Walk."

"We could play again," he said, his voice filled with depth and density. "Look where we are. Surrounded by immortal creatures who defied the gods." She drank in the comfort of his nearness, yearning to give in to his request, but fearful of gossipmongers and the repercussions of the last game they played. "Say you will divert yourself with me one more time." *Only one more?* Her heart sank into her chest then levitated as he crushed his mouth to hers and set her mind into a wild swirl. A shudder passed through her as their lips parted. "Will it be truth or a dare this time, Thenie?"

She blinked, combating the pressure of what others might think once they found out she'd been alone with Wright-Smythe in Elgin's room . . . of what the gossip would do to her family, her sisters. She fought the reality of right and wrong, of what Society deemed proper, digging deep into her heart for the truth.

She inhaled a breath of utter astonishment, longing to hear him speak her nickname once more. "I prefer a dare."

"A dare?" His hands dropped to his sides, a look of dejection taking hold. "I thought . . . I thought once you'd seen the Marbles, you would share my passion. Love them as much as I do. Desire to rescue them from the likes of Elgin and his kind. But even now, you refuse to acknowledge the truth." He peered at her intently, rubbing his thumb over her cheek. "I thought you knew. I thought you understood. You and I are the same."

But they weren't. She was a viscount's daughter. What hope did she have of marrying a man of his lowly profession? Did it matter? It would to Papa. She shook her head, sadly. "We are not the same, Mr. Wright-Smythe."

"Spencer."

"Spencer," she said, enjoying the way his given name tumbled from her lips. She buried her face in his throat and trailed her fingers over his muscular back, clinging to him, aching for him, knowing within her heart of hearts that she loved him as she'd never loved another. Drugged by that revelation, she allowed the embrace to continue for several moments before bringing it to an end.

He misunderstood her. Perhaps he always would. Goodness knows she'd hardly known herself when they'd first met. However, as she drew back, their gazes locked, his dismayed, hers tempted by the magnitude of her desire.

"Spencer." *I belong with you.* "I dare you to marry me."

EPILOGUE

Despina arrived in good fashion, dictating a passion with the gayest air imaginable. Nothing but skill carries a woman practicing her art on a man of merit and fortune. When a man meets encouragement, and her eyes come his way, repeating several significant looks, the happy fellow returns to his lodging, full of pleasant images; his brain dilated, and his spirit taken to the seat of pleasure. Twenty can speak eloquently, and a thousand dress genteelly, but gazing skillfully at a man requires firm resolve, as does striving to avoid the flaring fool attentive to her charms. Consider and compare yourselves to all that passes within view and observation. A man prepossessed experiences an assemblage of affection, hope, and a sense of success, but ultimately will lose, his natural wit sacrificed to Despina's heart and all its folds.

—The Morning Post

Three months later . . .

"AND HOW ARE you today, Mrs. Wright-Smythe?" Spencer drew back the curtains, his flawless body the living, breathing representation of Dionysos, reminding her of the intimate moments they'd shared in Elgin's room at the British Museum.

Light spilled into their bedchamber, revealing the sun rising over the Acropolis. "Come hither and I shall show you."

He stretched, every muscle in his back flexing, his buttocks tautening, filling her head with sensual imaginings. Oh, but he was magnificent, and the warmth radiating between her legs testified to that fact, making her desire mount. If she'd known they would enjoy each other's bodies in such a manner when they'd first met, she might have played the game differently from the start, spending less time daring to repel him and more time telling him the truth about her feelings. But there they were, living in a villa, Baros, his assistant, had secured. It was a smart little cottage with a small staff, and she was grateful for their humble home. Extremely happy, even if being with Spencer meant not seeing her parents, her sisters, or her cousins. Unlike her mother, she'd been given a chance to join her relic hunter—something she'd sworn never to do. In exchange, her husband appreciated her sacrifice and the daring she'd shown by traveling with him to the continent where she was a full partner in his vocation to save as many of Athens's antiquities as humanly possible.

"I thought we would investigate the caves devoted to Zeus, Apollo, Pan, Aphrodite, Eros, and Aglauros today. They are located on a small rocky hill, but especially important this time of year, because Aglauros ran off the cliff to save Athens. Her sacrifice is one of the reasons the festival is celebrated every year."

"Like Aglauros,"—she lowered the linens covering her body and posed like the woman she'd seen in Mrs. Dove-Lyon's painting—"I will do anything for my king."

"Your—" He reacted to her husky tone, looking over his shoulder at her like Lord Lansdowne's Herakles. "I am no king. I advise you to remember that."

"But you have a loyal liege."

"I do?" he asked, turning playful, his blue eyes darkening to sapphires. "And who, pray tell, may that be?" He put his hands on his hips, challenging her to defy him. "You?"

"No." She breathed lightly between parted lips, longing to tease him with abandon. Their passion soared when they battled wits. The pleasure they experienced made more persuasive by the fires they lit inside each other. She sank into the drowsy warmth of their bed. "Baros."

"Admit it." He turned to face her in all his naked glory, the sight of him never failing to astound her. "You enjoy teasing me."

"I am only speaking the truth."

He winked, taking a step closer to the bed. "This time."

She pried the end of the sheet free with her toe, raising the linens ever so slowly and thrilling at the change in his expression when he figured out what she was about. "I am not the only one who decided not to tell the truth."

"In what lifetime?" he asked, incredulous.

Her love for him deepened and intensified. He knew exactly what she meant. "If it wasn't for my cousins, I might never have known you are not who you say you are."

"I am more than a relic hunter. I'm your husband."

"A worthy calling. But you are, also, Baron Kilverstone."

He shrugged as if the moniker held little significance.

Sounds of the market filling with merchants and patrons drifted from below. Like them, Athens was waking up too. Here and there, an occasional wagon and horses trotted by. A bird sang, trilling out a sonnet, and children laughed as they set out to do their chores.

"I killed men to earn that title." The wounds of war went deep, and never deeper than upon the shoulders of the men who ran counterintelligence for the Admiralty. "I do not deserve it."

"The king thought differently." She rose from the bed, allowing the linens to fall from her figure into a pool at her feet. "As do I." She wrapped her arms around him and kissed him, stroking the rigid tendons on the back of his neck to help him relax. "We all admire your bravery and brilliance. My cousins. My parents. My sisters." She laughed in spite of herself, still holding onto one important secret. Mrs. Bessie Dove-Lyon. "You could not have made any of them happier to hear that your wedding gift included a large manse."

"Wartime recompense, nothing more."

"Nothing more? You are responsible for tenants and local workers who rely on your generosity."

"I am aware." He kissed her soundly. "And I will take care of the estate. But whatever you do, do not tell, Baros. I beg you." He seared a path of kisses down her neck. Currents of desire kindled within her, the glorious pulses settling between her legs. "If he finds out, he will make my life a living hell."

She arched into him, inspiring his tormented groan. "Does he have something against British barons?" she asked as his hands moved gently down her back and his kisses dipped lower, every kissing point a promise and a whisper of love.

"Because he'll expect to get paid more than he already does."

"And how am I to be paid for my devotion?" Her lips instinctively found their way to his mouth.

"Like this." A man of few words, Spencer showed her how rare and robust he really was—the sensuousness of his touch, his kiss, and the tremor leading her to an outcry of delight yielding to ecstasy. In the aftermath of their lovemaking, they lay together as was their habit, their limbs intertwined, the heat of passion fading as the sun scorched the landscape.

The rightness of the moment and all of the other moments they'd shared struck her. Her blood soared as she glanced at Spencer's sketch book. Its pages lay open on the desk by the window, where a breeze unsettled the drawings, flipping them over, one by one, until the sketch of her posing nude in Elgin's room appeared.

"You do not plan to take me to the king's cave today, do you?"

He chuckled and nibbled her ear. "Today, I dare you to kiss me in the temple of Athena. There is a code of mythic sacrifice there."

"You expect me to sacrifice a tour of the king's caves for Athena's temple?" She tried to act shocked. "While the citizens celebrate the festival of her birth?"

"The Panathenaea only happens once a year," he said matter-of-factly. "Sheep and cows are sacrificed and eaten the last day with competitions and a procession taking place."

It was an intricate ceremony and there was no way to know if she would be available to witness another one. So much could happen in a year, like Lottie and Grey reuniting and getting married and bringing Spencer back to England to meet her.

She pushed her breasts against the hardness of his chest and grinned when he moaned, rising up on her elbows to kiss his mouth. "It sounds adventurous."

"You are not upset about the caves?" he asked as if in acute physical pain.

She shook her head, desperate for him to believe her. "Lead me, and I will follow."

"I am done with dares," he assured her with a quivering, tentative touch. "I want the truth."

"Always." His sweet plea intoxicated her and a shiver of want took hold. "I love you, Lord Kilverstone."

A deep feeling of peace settled over her as he said, "I love you too, Lady Kilverstone."

He kissed her softly, closing his eyes for a moment. She studied his profile and smiled, basking in the idea that she had not settled for a marriage of convenience. No. She *had* married for love, and it was for that reason that she prayed for the same circumstance for her beloved sisters. She wasn't worried about the outcome, though she knew her sisters would go kicking and screaming to the altar since they wanted another Season.

One thing persuaded her not to worry about the future as she laid her head on Spencer's chest. She was not a gambler, however, she had, not one, but two aces up her sleeve.

Lottie and Mrs. Bessie Dove-Lyon.

The End

About the Author

Addicted to history and romance, Katherine Bone spent the better part of her childhood roaming the globe as an Army brat. Then while attending college, she was swept off her feet by a military officer. Yes, reader she married him, and they continued traveling the world. Four children, two Labradors and three cats later, Katherine put down roots in the south. Where, at last, she pursued her lifelong passion of creating vivid stories that came calling with abandon. Adventure. Mayhem. Swashbuckling heroes. Her books are pure escapism at heart.

Printed in Great Britain
by Amazon

43335372R00086